THE MARINE

NOVELIZATION BY

RUDY JOSEPHS

STORY BY MICHELL GALLAGHER

SCREENPLAY BY MICHELL GALLAGHER

AND ALAN MCELROY

POCKET BOOKS

New York   London   Toronto   Sydney

POCKET BOOKS, a division of Simon & Schuster, Inc.
1230 Avenue of the Americas, New York, NY 10020

This book is a work of fiction. Names, characters, places, and incidents are products of the author's imagination or are used fictitiously. Any resemblance to actual events or locales or persons, living or dead, is entirely coincidental.

ISBN-13: 978-1-4516-3184-5

This Pocket Books paperback edition September 2006

10 9 8 7 6 5 4 3 2 1

POCKET and colophon are registered trademarks of Simon & Schuster, Inc.

Cover design by John Vairo, Jr

Visit us on the World Wide Web
http://www.simonsays.com
http://www.wwe.com

Manufactured in the United States of America

For information regarding special discounts for bulk purchases, please contact Simon & Schuster Special Sales at 1-800-456-6798 or business@simonandschuster.com.

For Harley

FILE: USMC-010172
LOCATION: Jakarta, Indonesia
MISSION: Four unidentified men have taken over the American Embassy in Jakarta. They are threatening to blow up the building, along with the captives inside.
OBJECTIVE: Free the hostages unharmed. Regain control of the embassy.
MISSION LEADER: Sergeant John Triton
STATUS: Complete. Control restored.
FRIENDLY CASUALTIES: 0

FILE: USMC-111372
LOCATION: Tikrit, Iraq
MISSION: A convoy of American aid workers has been kidnapped. The kidnappers demand to exchange the hostages for Iraqi criminals being held for war crimes. One hostage has already been executed.
OBJECTIVE: Free remaining hostages unharmed. Neutralize threat.
MISSION LEADER: Sergeant John Triton
STATUS: Complete. Threat neutralized.
FRIENDLY CASUALTIES: 0

FILE: USMC-011373
LOCATION: Pavlodar, Kazakhstan
MISSION: The facilities of an American oil company operating in Kazakhstan have been taken under siege by Russian separatists. The separatists are protesting the transfer of ownership from the now incarcerated Yevgeny Mislovec to the American corporation. The chief officers of the com-

pany have been killed. The separatists claim they will kill the rest of the hostages, one by one, until the company agrees to relinquish ownership to the separatists and return to the U.S.

OBJECTIVE: Free remaining captives unharmed. Regain control of the facility.

MISSION LEADER: Sergeant John Triton

STATUS: Complete. Threat neutralized.

FRIENDLY CASUALTIES: 0

FILE: USMC-111473

LOCATION: NW Frontier Province—Afghanistan/Pakistan Border

MISSION: Three Marines on a routine scout have been ambushed and taken by an Al Qaeda militant group. The group has claimed responsibility for a gruesome series of recent beheadings, and they have threatened to continue their cause with the current hostages.

OBJECTIVE: Gather intelligence of location and exact number of hostiles. Secure position and wait for supplemental forces.

MISSION LEADER: Sergeant John Triton

STATUS: In progress . . .

1

Sergeant John Triton looked out over the dark desolate landscape below him. He could see dim lights off in the distance, but little else. He heard nothing but the sound of the rushing wind. This was the dangerous part of the mission. Some would say the entire operation was dangerous. Some would say it was a suicide mission. Some did, in fact. But John Triton wasn't about to die. He was simply doing what had to be done.

The rushing air blew past him as he waited. He'd traditionally pull his chute at two thousand feet. If he was in a playful mood, maybe seventeen-fifty. But tonight he'd wait until he was only fifteen hundred feet from the ground. The difference between the three heights was mere seconds, but those seconds were also the difference between life and death.

Triton checked his altimeter and waited. His mind went blank. On a mission like this, he tried not to think of anything but the job. He wasn't worried about the fall. He didn't care about the enemy. And he especially refused to think of his beautiful wife, Kate, back at home, because if anything would distract him, it would be that.

At fifteen hundred feet Triton pulled the ripcord, sending the black parachute billowing out of his pack. It slowed him only slightly, as the momentum he had built was still carrying him quickly to the ground. He allowed himself a brief flash of concern. *Did I wait too long to pull the cord?*

Triton quickly wiped that thought from his mind. For three Marines, he was the only hope of rescue. He would complete his mission even if he shattered his legs upon landing and had to drag himself to the compound.

He hit the ground in under a minute. The landing was hard, but not too painful. More to the point, he had managed to evade detection. The lack of shouts and shooting told him that. Not that he expected anything to happen; infrared had shown him that he was at least a mile away from any signs of human life before he'd jumped.

Even though both he and the parachute were all in black and the jump occurred on a moonless night, there had still been a risk. Anyone on watch with a good set of night-vision binoculars could have made him out. That person only had to be looking into the sky at the right angle. It wasn't as if that scenario was entirely out of the question. Terrorists nowadays were surprisingly well funded and usually had the newest in surveillance technology before the U.S. Marine Corps could get hold of it. The level of risk had been acceptable as far as Triton was concerned.

But the jump was in the past, and Triton wasn't

thinking of the past as he removed his pack and bundled up his chute. He quickly dug a shallow hole in the sand and dropped the chute inside, throwing sand over it to keep it covered for the time being. By the time anyone stumbled across the parachute in the middle of the desert, he would be long gone.

He dropped his night-vision goggles over his eyes and surveyed the landscape. The goggles gave a dark green tint to the world around him. Out in the middle of the desert there was little ambient light for the goggles to pick up, which made the few lights off in the distance even more distinguishable. The compound wasn't large, but it was easily seen from the air during the day. Due to its location, any approach while the sun was up was impossible.

Once Triton confirmed that the area was clear, he began his mile-long hike to the compound. He was well versed at running through the desert at night by now. Years of practice had taught him how to be aware of nighttime predators. Most of the animals that came out after dark weren't a threat to someone his size. It was the land itself that was the problem, littered as it was with bumps and burrows. A man could easily hurt himself if he had not honed his skills of observation.

Triton ripped the goggles off as he approached the compound. The flames rising from the barrels placed at various intervals across the desert ground made the glasses unnecessary. Unsurprisingly, the place seemed low-tech from the outside, but he knew that there was enough jamming equipment on the premises to make it impossible to get a clear read from the sky on the number of people inside. He only hoped that he'd be able to get a comm signal out. If the terrorists were that well funded for equipment, Triton could only imagine the kinds of weaponry he would encounter.

Oddly, there was no one guarding the perimeter. It didn't take long for Triton to realize why. Two video cameras were stationed on the high wall around the compound. He considered it surprisingly light security, especially considering it was no problem for him to sneak by them unnoticed. Once inside, he waited for sounds of alarm, but there were none. The cameras continued to scan the night desert, uselessly.

The compound consisted of four ramshackle buildings of varying sizes spread out over the area, surrounding one large building in the rear that looked the most formidable of the bunch, which wasn't saying much. It seemed likely that that building would be the one where the action was taking place, but Triton needed to check them all out first. Moving from building to building, he easily confirmed his suspicions that they were empty. Still, he didn't like it.

Unconfirmed intel had indicated that there might be an underground bunker on the compound. Triton's new commanding officer, Major Wilson, hadn't lent much credence to that report. Far less, in fact, than Triton would have liked. He had been through enough of these missions to know that he had to expect the unexpected. It wasn't like he was about to just ignore the possibility that there was another unseen part to the compound.

Although "building" was a rather generous term for the shack he was standing beside, Triton considered entering it. Surveying the area, he realized that if there was a bunker, it wouldn't be under the main building. That was too much of a target. It would be under one of the outer buildings. He knew that he was on a timetable, but that wasn't as important as securing the area. As such, he decided to give another attempt at reasoning with his superior officer.

Triton confirmed that the area wasn't currently under surveillance. No one was within earshot to hear his communications. There was what he considered an acceptable risk for him to make contact. He switched on his radio, hoping that the signal could break through any interference.

"This is Ghost Two reporting in," Triton said into the comm.

"Are you in position?" Major Wilson responded.

"Negative," Triton replied. "Have conducted preliminary surveillance of outer buildings. Request permission for further reconnaissance to verify unconfirmed intel."

"Negative," Major Wilson replied. *"Proceed with mission."*

Triton was disgusted by the major's shortsightedness. He needed to confirm that there weren't going to be any surprises when the choppers came in.

He tried again: "Request permission—"

"*Negative!*" Major Wilson shouted into the comm much more loudly than necessary. "*Proceed with mission. We don't have time for any of your flights of fancy.*"

Triton didn't know what the hell the major was talking about. He didn't particularly care for the man's tone or his odd choice of words either. He couldn't believe he was taking orders from some desk jockey who had recently been transferred to the field and didn't know anything more than what was written in the training manuals.

The problem was that he *was* taking orders. As much as Triton hated this part of the job, he was a Marine. He was sent in to do a mission. There was no time for debate.

"Understood," he said through clenched teeth as he switched off the radio.

Triton took one last look at the small outer shacks before moving toward the main building. As he crossed the compound, he saw two guards stationed outside the door. They did not look like much of a threat, but taking the guards out so soon was too big a risk without knowing who was in the room.

Triton made his approach, careful of the exterior guards. Now that he knew the location of the objective, he could set up surveillance from outside the building. Slipping around to the side, he found the thin walls would be perfect for his needs.

He bent down to his knees and took his tools out of the pack he had slid off of his back. He slipped three metal rods together into a makeshift hand drill. Finding an especially weak point in the construction at the base of the building, he started to drill a small hole into the wood. It only took a few seconds before he could see light spilling out from the inside. He put away the small hand drill and took out a video camera.

Slipping a cable through the hole, Triton worked the controls on the video machine to adjust the angle on the camera at the other end of the cable. With the controls, he was able to send the cable snaking up the wall slightly to get a better shot as he turned on the video screen.

The screen rippled. A dropout line cut across the darkness, followed by static. Eventually, a grainy video image flickered on, revealing a grim scene. Three Special Forces Marines were sitting on the floor with their hands tied behind them. Their faces were covered with cuts and bruises. Even on the rough video, Triton could see that they were exhausted.

Seven terrorists wearing black balaclava masks were lording it over the prisoners. The leader held a machete defiantly over the head of one of the captives. He was spewing some propaganda into a video camera held by an eighth terrorist.

Triton didn't know what the terrorist was saying, but he could probably figure it out. The speeches were always the same, decrying the "infidel foreigners" who "rob the riches of their country."

He recognized the voice from the tapes he had listened to while prepping for the mission. It was Mohammed Abgaryan, just as his superiors had suspected. Abgaryan had been recently making a name for himself with a series of beheadings of journalists and civilian security agents. He had made similar speeches on video, broadcasting the taped murders via the Internet. These were the first American Marines he had managed to capture. As a result, Abgaryan's rhetoric seemed to be kicked up a notch. The megalomaniacal ramblings betrayed a distinct joy at the terrorists' presumed good fortune.

Little did the militants realize that capturing Marines was to be the worst thing they could have done for their cause. And for their own lives.

Triton focused his own miniature camera on the Marines. They were strong men. Special Forces were among the best of the best. But even Triton could understand the fear he saw in their eyes. They did not know if help was on the way. They did not know that John Triton was just on the other side of the wall.

The confirmed intel, at least, had been correct. Seven terrorists were in the room. Numbers eight and nine stood outside the door. Those rumors about the bunker were still a concern, but Triton couldn't do much about that. He was already later than he would have liked to be in making contact with the count confirmation.

He surveyed the room through the camera as well as eyeballing the building from the outside. The priority was to get the three prisoners out of the room safely; he could keep an eye out for the bunker later. The last thing he needed was an extra detail of terrorists interfering with the rescue.

Triton shut down the monitor. He checked around him to confirm he was still alone. There weren't any cameras back here, as far as he could tell. The guards to the building were still a safe distance away around front. Once again he turned on his radio.

Triton whispered into his head mike. "Ghost Two in position. Intel confirmed. Nine hostiles and three Marines."

"*Copy that, Ghost Two,*" replied the voice of Major Wilson. "*Your extraction will be at Oh-One-Hundred.*"

Screams drew Triton's attention away from the communication. Well-trained Marines did not shout like that without reason. The agony was heart-stopping. Triton froze. He could hear Abgaryan's voice grow louder as he continued spewing his rhetoric. The man was gearing up to make his statement; the one without words.

Triton knew what had to be done.

"Negative," he said back into the comm. The men inside could not wait.

"*Ghost Two, you are not to engage,*" Wilson said. "*Repeat: Do not engage. Alpha team is on the way. Pull back.*"

"No time," Triton said. Another scream indicated that they were already wasting more time than they had. Not checking the buildings for a reported secret bunker was one thing. He wasn't just going to sit back while three Marines lost their lives.

"*Pull back, Ghost Two,*" Wilson insisted. "*That is a direct order. Wait for—*"

Triton yanked out his earpiece and moved toward the screams.

Triton knew better than to go bursting into the room. Even though time was short, he would be no good to the Marines inside if he died before he could rescue them. So he waited, but only for the right moment to present itself.

As Triton waited for his moment, one of the guards left his station. *Maybe he doesn't have the stomach for what's ahead.* Triton didn't care. He stepped back into the shadows as the man passed and continued toward one of the side buildings. One less enemy to worry about for the moment.

Triton could hear the propaganda that the terrorists were spewing inside the room. He still couldn't translate the language, but the anger had ratcheted up another notch. Triton didn't need to know what the man was saying to get the gist from the volume of his words. The deaths would be starting soon. Little did they know that it wasn't the prisoners who would be dying.

Once Triton was sure that the lone terrorist was inside the other building, he emerged from the darkness. The remaining guard was focused on closing the door on the screams. Triton's chance had come.

He rushed the guard as the man turned. Triton threw an elbow to the man's chin, knocking him cold and sending his gun clattering to the ground.

The chatter in the room stopped. They were probably wondering about the noise outside. The damn gun had to fall—Triton would punish himself for that later. Someone would be coming out soon enough to check on the guard. Triton had lost the element of surprise, but he knew how he could get it back.

He lifted the guard's unconscious body and threw it through the already battered wooden door.

The door imploded, sending splinters of wood in every direction. There was no time to think as he followed the body into the room. Triton was moving purely on instinct, barely pausing to take stock of the situation.

The Marines were still alive. They looked both relieved and terrified as they saw John Triton's black-painted face as he entered the area. Surely they would have heard of him. He knew his name was whispered among the rank and file in a mixture of awe, respect, and maybe even some fear. John Triton, Virtuoso of Violence . . . avenging Michelangelo of Death.

At least, that's what he had heard.

The Al Qaeda leader, Mohammed Abgaryan, had a machete poised above the nearest captive's neck. Triton had been right in thinking there was no time to spare. His unexpected entrance had likely saved the man's life. He'd have to remember to bring that up to Major Wilson if any questions came up over his actions.

But he was no longer thinking. He was like a man possessed. A killer instinct was raging inside him. A fierce, almost animalistic hunger was bubbling up from within his soul.

The cameraman recording the event for a future webcast turned his camera to the direction of the noise. Triton gave him something worth filming as he fired a single shot at the man. The bullet hit its mark, slamming into the man's head and killing him instantly. The man dropped to the floor, with his camera falling beside him. Triton almost wished that the terrorists were broadcasting the images live. There would be no better way to send the message not to mess with American Marines.

Abgaryan pushed the prisoner's face down to the ground and charged Triton with his machete, screaming, *"Allah hu akbar!"*

Triton holstered his pistol, then raised his machine gun and began firing on the leader. The bullets struck the bastard squarely in the chest, knocking him off his feet and pitching him backward to the ground. His machete dropped to the ground during the fall.

Triton's rounds continued to strafe the walls in front of him, hitting an unmarked container. The barrel exploded, setting off a massive fireball that engulfed the bodies of the two nearest terrorists in flames. Now the screams of horror were coming from a different source as the two men flailed about in the fire.

Before Triton could get off more shots, another terrorist came at him with a combat knife, slashing Triton's arm. Pain shot through him right up his shoulder, causing him to drop the machine gun. It fell to the ground along with some of his blood. Triton barely registered the injury. He had more important concerns at the moment.

Another Al Qaeda operative joined his buddy, and the two men faced off against Triton. They were both armed with knives, but they weren't the only ones who had come prepared. Triton slid his hands down to his belt and pulled out his own knife, readying himself for close-quarter combat. He had been through worse. However, this one had the additional challenge of one enemy who was right-handed while the other was left. It made the defensive maneuvering slightly different, but far from impossible for an experienced Marine like Triton.

Righty attacked first, leading with his knife. It was a stupid move. Triton swung into the man's attacking arm and nearly knocked the knife free. The attacker maintained his balance and punched with his weaker hand. Triton easily held off the blows and the renewed knife attack.

As they fought, the other man charged Triton, mistakenly believing the Marine was distracted. Triton kicked the new attacker in the chest, sending the man backward. Triton then used his momentum to spin and jam his knife into the neck of his first assailant.

The downside to that maneuver was that when the

terrorist pulled away, choking in his own blood, he had also taken Triton's knife with him. Triton assumed the terrorist would have preferred not to have it in him in the first place but, in battle, people didn't always get what they wanted.

One of the other terrorists, still alight in flame from the earlier explosion, refused to go down. Motivated by either faith or stupidity, he went for Triton with flames trailing behind him. Triton picked up the man's fiery body and tossed it across the room. It continued right through the wall, the flames refusing to subside.

In the brief moment of distraction, the man Triton had dubbed "Lefty" rushed up behind Triton again and cut a nasty slash in his back. Triton jumped forward to prevent further injury and saw that he no longer needed his combat knife. The militant leader's machete was lying only a few feet in front of him.

Triton dove for the machete, grabbed it off the floor, and completed a roll to bring himself back to his feet. Spinning, he saw Lefty and another man rushing him. He blocked the first knife blow from Lefty with the tip of the machete he held in his hand. But the second attack from the other enemy landed across his arm, cutting into it deeply.

Triton raged on despite the pain. Swinging the machete, he cut a wide swath through the air and then through both of the terrorists. Their deaths were painful, but quick. Triton watched as their bodies slowly fell to the floor.

By Triton's count, the fight was over, but the Al

Qaeda leader refused to die. He lashed out one last time, screaming with the howl of a wounded animal. He raised his pistol to fire at Triton, but before he could get the shot off, Triton dropped the man with his own machete.

Blood sprayed Triton's black-painted face. Abgaryan was dying. Abgaryan's death wasn't part of his initial mission profile, but it was a satisfying conclusion anyway. Triton jammed his steel-tipped boot down on the man, snapping his neck.

Silence.

Triton stood in the center of the room, surrounded by bodies. The USMC prisoners were looking at him with shocked faces. He knew what they were silently asking themselves. He'd heard many others mumbling it after similar rescue missions. They wondered if what they had just seen was true. They were questioning whether or not it was a dream. They would probably continue to doubt that it had happened for months, if not years.

Triton dropped the machete and retrieved his knife from the neck of one of the dead terrorists. He used the man's clothes to wipe the blood off the blade, then cut each of the hostages free.

The three soldiers stocked up on their captives' weapons, jamming in fresh clips as the bodies of the Al Qaeda terrorists lay dead around them.

Outside the building Triton heard a familiar sound. Two HCH53-E Super Stallion helicopters were approaching the coordinates. The sound was quickly followed by gunfire from the ground. Then they heard massive return fire back from the helicopters.

By Triton's estimation, he had taken out eight of the nine terrorists on-site. Apparently the unconfirmed intel had been correct. There was a bunker under the compound. All that ground fire couldn't be coming from one man.

Triton looked at the Marines. They weren't out of this yet.

"Can everyone move?" Triton asked. They were beaten, but none of their injuries looked debilitating. Triton could probably get them out of there on his own, but he would need both of his hands and couldn't stop to carry anyone.

The three men nodded that they would be fine. Triton expected no less from the Marines. They were young, but he could tell that they were already battle-scarred like him. He imagined that being taken prisoner had hardened them even more. It was the one good thing about their capture—they would need that strength to get them through the next few minutes.

"Sir, what's the best way out of here?" the youngest one asked.

Triton locked and loaded his HK-MP5 before turning back to face the men. "Behind me."

He led the men out of the building behind the staccato burst of machine-gun fire, explosions, and the sound of helicopters.

About a dozen terrorists were spilling out of one of the smaller outbuildings, the one that the guy Triton had seen earlier had gone into. There must have been a trapdoor leading to the secret room in there, because Triton hadn't seen anything during his cursory recon earlier. He silently cursed Major Wilson, though there wasn't anything that could have been done. Had Triton gone to check the small buildings, the Marines would surely have died before he could get to them.

But that was a debate for another time. The compound in front of him was exploding in gunfire and screams. Two choppers were hovering above, looking for a clear spot to land. Triton knew that the only clearing was outside the high walls of the compound. There were only about a dozen terrorists between him and his escape. With three Marines getting his back, Triton didn't think it would even be a fair fight—for the terrorists.

Triton took a break from firing and threw his arm forward, giving the signal to move out. Two terrorists had dropped during his initial attack coming through the door. Triton continued firing as he reached for a grenade in his belt. He pulled the pin and threw it at the small building, causing an explosion that collapsed the building in on itself. If there was anyone else inside, they wouldn't be coming out any time soon.

The terrorists nearest the building all dropped from the blast, but about half of them got back on their feet and kept firing. Between the chopper fire and the Marines on the ground, they would be mowed down soon enough.

Once the other Al Qaeda had gotten back to their

feet, they renewed the attack. Triton and the former captives were three-quarters of the way to the outer wall. Everything slowed for a moment as a bullet breezed by Triton and struck one of the Marines in the leg. The man fell hard.

"Cover me," Triton yelled to the other two.

The men quickly jumped between him and the terrorists, firing wildly at them. Triton picked up the fallen Marine, flung the guy over his shoulder, and resumed firing. All twelve of the terrorists were dead by the time Triton and the other Marine reached the wall.

Triton considered waving good-bye to the security cameras on his way out, but decided against it. He figured that there was probably no one left to monitor the image on the other end anyway. He carried the Marine out to the landing chopper, and all four of them boarded.

"He took one in the leg!" Triton yelled to the medic as he laid the wounded man out on the floor of the helicopter.

He moved out of the way to let the medic do his job, but the wounded Marine grabbed at Triton's arm, not letting him go.

Triton leaned back to him. "You're gonna be okay. Let the medic take care of you."

There was no fear in the Marine's eyes, only respect. "Thank you, sir," the Marine said as he saluted Triton. It was clear that the man was holding back tears.

Triton moved to the back of the helicopter, surprised to find that Major Wilson had come along for the ride.

Triton had suspected the man was overseeing the mission from a comfortable chair at the staging area.

Wilson was not looking at him with esteem or admiration in his eyes. "I gave you a direct order," he said. "You were not to engage the enemy."

"If I hadn't, these men would be dead," Triton answered.

"That was not your call to make," Wilson replied.

"Well, someone had to make it," Triton said, going toe-to-toe with the major. "The same person that should have made the call for a complete recon of the area."

As the chopper lifted off, the two men stared at each other threateningly.

"Consider yourself on report," Major Wilson said.

"If that's all, *Major*," Triton said, "I'm just going to sit back here and continue bleeding, if you don't mind."

Triton didn't wait for an answer as he pushed past the man and headed for the back of the helicopter. He wished he had a bigger place to get away from the jackass. Triton knew the medics should look at his wounds too, but they were busy with the Marine who had been shot. The cuts still ached, but it was nothing compared to the anger burning inside him, which was directed solely at the major.

3

Kate Triton sat in the break room of University Hospital of South Carolina, trying to cram a semester's worth of biochem into a half hour lunch. Between her seemingly endless nursing shifts and attending medical school full-time, she hardly had any time to keep up with her studies. With finals coming, she had a tremendous amount of catching up to do if she was going to continue with the program. Her grades weren't really the problem, it was mostly the time commitment. At least she didn't have to worry about a social life with John away, God knows where.

She tried to push thoughts of her husband out of her mind. Thinking about him was a surefire way to avoid learning or retaining the information she so desperately needed to absorb. But she couldn't help that her mind would continually drift to thoughts of him throughout the day. It was bad enough that his life as a Marine took him away from her for so long, but what was worse was that she never knew where he was. Considering the current state of global conflicts, she didn't want to think about any of it.

Even though Kate had known that John was a Marine when she married him, she never really understood what it would be like to be a Marine's wife until she'd become one. Not that she regretted the decision for a moment. She knew John. He was doing what he needed to do. She understood that. But the knowledge didn't make it easier every time he had to say goodbye.

She shook her head vigorously, physically trying to stop herself from going down this road once again. Studying was what she was supposed to be doing, not thinking of John. That was just one of those things that was easier said than done.

Kate did manage to push John from her thoughts for a few minutes to make some headway in her reading. It wasn't like she was really far behind. She saw examples of her biochem studies every day in her nursing duties. All she had to do with her reading was learn how the information would apply to her future career as a doctor.

"Hey, Kate," her friend and coworker Carol said as she came into the break room.

"Please don't tell me Mister Davidson is asking for me again," Kate said in frustration. "If he calls me 'the little blond nursey' one more time, I'm going to accidentally misplace his bedpan and forget to answer his page when he calls."

"Oh, I've taken care of Davidson," Carol said with a laugh. "I've scheduled Jorge to give him his next sponge bath."

Kate laughed as well. Jorge was a considerably large

orderly who was probably one of the nicest guys she'd ever known, but certainly not the person Mister Davidson would want sponging him down.

"I'd almost want to be there to see the look on Davidson's face when Jorge comes into the room," Kate said. "But I've got studying to do."

"I know," Carol said, "but you've also got a call."

"Can you please take a message?" Kate asked. "I've got to get through this chapter."

"Do I look like your receptionist?" Carol joked. "Anything you want me to type up for you while I'm at it?"

"Please?" Kate pleaded. "This is important."

"Okay," Carol said, continuing to poke fun at Kate. "I get it. You're going to be some big important doctor. Have to keep us nurses in our place. Fine. I'll take a message. Probably not important anyway. Just some guy who says he's your husband."

Kate forgot all about her book and jumped out of her seat. "John? John's on the phone? Why didn't you say something?"

"I thought I just did," Carol said.

Kate hardly heard her friend as she, Kate, ran through the door and down to the nurses' station.

"Line three," Carol called after her.

Kate reached the station, bypassing the desk to go to the small private office in back. The head nurse didn't like them taking personal calls, but Kate was on her break, and—really—who was going to have a problem with her talking to her Marine husband, cur-

25

rently stationed abroad serving their country? She'd actually like to see someone raise a stink about it. That would make a great story on the eleven o'clock news.

The light on line three was blinking about as quickly as Kate's heart was beating. She took a moment to compose herself before she answered, but then realized it was pointless and picked up the receiver.

"John?" she said with excitement.

"Hey, honey," he replied. "How's my future doctor?"

"Missing you more and more every day," she replied, hoping she didn't sound like one of those needy wives, but realizing she didn't really care if she did.

Just hearing his voice was enough to toss all logic out the window. They hadn't spoken in over a month and hadn't seen each other since the semester had started. Sure, there were always e-mails. He dropped her a line as often as he could, but there was never any regularity to their correspondence because he was always going off for one mission or another. And even when he did write, he couldn't really tell her anything specific, like even where he was.

Hearing his voice live on the line was different. For one thing, she could immediately tell that something was wrong, even though he had hardly said much more than a simple greeting. That kind of thing she couldn't pick up on e-mail.

"I didn't interrupt anything, did I?" he asked almost timidly. As if he was afraid of bothering her. This was not the John that she knew.

"Nope," she replied, wanting to give him a chance to get to the problem before she forced it out of him. "I'm on break. You have great timing."

"It's those video cameras I secretly placed before I left," he said in a halfhearted attempt at a joke. "I'm keeping an eye on you so I know when to call."

"Then it's so nice of you to wait and not interrupt me when I'm with my boyfriend at the house," she played him right back.

"Yeah," John continued, but Kate could tell that his heart really wasn't in it. "I should mention I took him out with some C-4 I placed under the foundation in case something like that happened. Just so you know, the house is pretty much gone too."

"John," Kate said, cutting to the chase. "What's wrong?"

"Well, my wife just admitted to having an affair," he went on.

"John," she insisted.

"There's been a bit of a situation," he said, meandering toward the subject.

If there's one thing a Marine's spouse can't stand, it's stalling. "What happened?" Kate asked, trying not to sound frightened. "Are you okay?"

"Oh, no, it's nothing like that," John replied. "I'm fine. Well . . . physically, there's nothing wrong with me."

Kate sat down on the desk, worried. Physical wounds she could handle. As long as John was able to talk to her, she'd be able to deal with any injury that he could bring home. But this sounded different. John wasn't big on opening up about his problems. Not that he was cold and closed off like his father had been. He just didn't like to worry her about the stuff going on inside his head. And that's where it sounded this conversation was going.

"What kind of situation are we talking about?" Kate asked.

"Well, I can't quite tell you," he said.

"Of course you can," she replied. "John, you can tell me anything."

"No, Kate," he said, struggling with his words. "I mean I *can't* tell you. What I can say is that I did something. Something that needed to be done. Something that I would do again . . . But, you see, I kind of disobeyed orders to do it."

"Oh, John," Kate said with concern, not disappointment. She knew John well enough to know that he wouldn't go around ignoring his superiors without a good reason. But still, the Marine Corps didn't look kindly on that kind of thing. "What's going on?"

"Well, I'm not quite sure right now," John said. "I've got someone working on my case."

"Your case?" Kate said before she could stop herself. Images of the brig filled her head. Not that she knew what a brig looked like, but she couldn't imagine it was a good thing.

"Now, I'm sure it's all going to work out," John said. She could tell he was trying to sound reassuring for himself as well as for her. "I know I was in the right. It's just . . . I don't know how it's gonna go yet."

"I'm here for you," Kate said. "Whatever you need. I love you, John."

"And I love you too, Kate," he replied. "But like I said, I know it's gonna turn out okay. I just wanted you to know. But I . . . I've used up my time. I've got to go."

"But—"

"I mean it," John said and she could hear the pain in his voice. "I love you."

"I know you do," she replied.

She held the receiver in her hand for a minute after she heard the call disconnect. She couldn't imagine how her husband was feeling at the moment. The Corps was his life. At times, she felt she ran a close second to it, but she knew that he did love her just a bit more. If he had disobeyed an order, of course, he had done it because it was the right thing to do. But that didn't make the situation any easier now. Not if it had gotten to a point where he had to call her to tell her about it. She could only wonder about what he wasn't telling her.

And yet a small part of her was relieved. An investigation meant that he was out of harm's way for the time being. He had never really been able to tell her about his missions, but she knew he wasn't sitting behind a desk pushing paperwork. John was out in the field. From what she did know, it was clear that he was often risking his life. She tried not to think about that. She also tried not to think about the fact that if he *did* get sent to the brig, that too would keep him safe.

She really hated herself for that last part. It was such a horrible thing to think. But horrible thoughts that came out of love weren't truly that bad. At least, that was how she justified it.

There was always the chance that he could be sent home. To have John with her would be wonderful for Kate, but she knew that it would be the worst thing in the world for John. He wasn't simply a career Marine. He was a *lifer*. Kate had already accepted that about him. It was even a part of the reason she fell in love with him. A man that committed to his calling could always show that same commitment to his relationship. She had been right about that, too.

As much as she knew that coming home would kill a part of John, she couldn't stop that tiny part of her heart from wishing that it might come true.

4

Triton had been out of commission far too long. It wasn't the wounds. They had been superficial. The stitches, the scars, they were nothing new. And they weren't what was keeping him from the action. It was the stupid bureaucracy.

Disobeying orders. As if that were the first time Triton had bent rules to get the job done. But this was a mission under the command of Major Wilson, the hotshot desk jockey bucking to get out of the field and back into the air-conditioned officers' club where he belonged. He had just managed to pull desert duty owing to the lack of command officers in the field. That's the problem when these things stretch on longer than expected. Lack of planning. And it's the grunts that pay for it.

At least he'd had the chance to speak to Kate. He hadn't been able to bring himself to say half the things that he wanted to say to her, but it just made him feel better to hear her voice. She had a way of putting things in perspective without even saying a word. The Corps was Triton's calling, but Kate was his life. Although right now, the Corps wasn't calling that much.

Triton was currently "stationed" at the USMC Second Battalion Command in Stuttgart, Germany. While it was true that any European base was under constant threat of terrorist attack, the most dangerous action Triton had seen since being sent there was a nasty paper cut.

To keep from going insane, Triton spent most of his time in the weight room surrounded by free weights, treadmills, and similarly bored Marines. The doctors had warned him against strenuous exercise until his wounds fully healed, but Triton didn't care. His body would be through a lot worse when he was back in the field. His stitches could take a little workout.

There was no doubt that Triton would be back at work soon. Even though he knew he had sounded a little unsure when he spoke with Kate, it was just a momentary doubt. These things had a way of working themselves out. He would be made an example for a while, then eventually his record would stand on its own. He would be vindicated, the charges would be dropped, and then he would be sent on another life-threatening mission to make up for the trouble. It was the way of the world as Triton knew it.

In the meantime, he had to keep in shape. Triton straddled the weight bench as he performed his reps. His tight tank top was drenched in sweat. He knew the other Marines were watching him. He felt their respect. But they'd keep their distance, sensing that he preferred it that way.

It was easier to do his job if he didn't think of these

men and women as friends. He had friends at home. He didn't need them here. The last thing Triton wanted was to mix personal feelings with a mission. Feelings would cloud his judgment. Emotions had already made him question orders. Of course, they had been stupid orders to begin with.

Triton pushed through his last few reps. The weights he was lifting totaled over three hundred pounds. The doctors *had* told him to take it easy, after all.

His muscles were bulging and straining against the stitches. His body was trembling with Herculean effort, but he refused to give in. He labored, unbowed, against the monumental weights.

The weights were getting harder and harder to press. Then, suddenly, something snapped inside him. His jaw set. His eyes burned. It was the same inner rage that fueled him in Afghanistan . . . in Iraq . . . and in all the other places he had been sent in when no one else could do the job.

With a gut-searing yell, he pushed the weights up over his head. He held them there, proving his dominance, before dropping them back on the rack. The room was silent. At first, Triton thought it was due to his yell, but he soon learned differently.

Around the room, soldiers dropped their weights as Colonel Braun entered the gym. Triton turned and snapped to attention, as did everyone around him. The colonel had been assigned to defend Triton against the charges that Wilson had brought.

Things hadn't looked good when Braun had taken the case. There were whispers about Triton spending time in the brig. In addition to the wounded Marine, one of the helicopters had suffered considerable damage in the firefight. It had barely made it back to the staging area.

At first, Triton was blamed for that too, since he had initiated the conflict. However, Braun had argued that Triton wanted to do more thorough recon to confirm that a dozen Al Qaeda weren't going to suddenly come bursting out of a building during the escape. At least they had dodged that bullet. All that stood afterward was the charge of disobeying orders.

Triton found it all a bit ridiculous, but Braun took everything very seriously. The guy was down-to-earth, and Triton liked him enough. He knew that Braun would get him off, clear his record, and probably make sure that Triton never crossed paths with the idiotic Wilson ever again.

"At ease, Marines," Braun announced to the room.

The Marines slightly relaxed their stances.

Triton locked eyes with the colonel, who was heading directly toward him. For some reason, the colonel was having trouble looking Triton directly in the eye. This was not a good sign. Neither was the envelope in the colonel's hand. Triton knew that it held his entire future.

"Outside," Braun told Triton brusquely. "Ten minutes."

Triton tried to ignore the tone in Braun's voice. He

almost sounded angry, which was not what Triton wanted to hear. It didn't bode well for the news that he was about to deliver. Triton imagined a permanent mark on his record. But even that wouldn't be the end of the world. He wasn't looking for a promotion anytime soon. Last thing he wanted was to move up the ranks and find himself stuck behind a desk with losers like Wilson.

Apparently, the other people had noticed the strained tone in Braun's voice as well. He could tell that they sensed that something was up. They all took special care to avoid his eyes as he left the room.

Triton made for the showers. He quickly rinsed off, dressed, and was headed outside in eight minutes flat. In life, as on missions, Triton didn't like to think of the future or worry about the past, but now he couldn't stop thinking of either as doubt crept into his mind over what was in that envelope.

He caught up with Colonel Braun, who was waiting for him on the steps out of the building. The colonel's manner had not lightened.

"We've approached it from every angle," the colonel said without pleasantries. "The judge advocate has heard your case."

"What about an appeal?" Triton asked. They had already been around a couple times. Triton had thought the options had been getting better. Apparently he was wrong. But still, there had to be another alternative—some course of action they had yet to try.

"They're not accepting any more appeals," the

colonel replied. "This is it, John. The State Department's calling the shots."

Triton had no clue why State would be involved—unless Wilson's connections had stretched further than anyone knew. He refused to believe that they had exhausted all their efforts. Not when his record was taken into consideration. People threw around the word *hero* far too much as far as Triton was concerned. He wasn't about to be one of them, especially when he was talking about himself. But Triton knew that his prior actions spoke volumes. With recruitment down and hostilities up, you just don't get rid of men like him.

Besides, he had just been doing his job. Granted, he had done more than he was instructed to do, but it all worked out in the end. Since when was saving three lives considered a failure?

"Colonel, I was there," he insisted. "I did what had to be done."

Braun didn't respond for a moment. He seemed torn.

"Off the record," he finally said, "I would have done exactly the same thing. But the bottom line is, you disobeyed a direct order."

"Those men would be dead if I'd followed orders," Triton said, knowing he didn't need to remind Braun. The colonel was on his side. There had to be a way out. "C'mon, Colonel. Just tell me what I need to do."

Triton stood waiting for the answer. He didn't care what it was; he was prepared to grovel before Wilson if it meant saving his position. John Triton was a Marine. He was the best. And he wasn't going to let some pissant little screw-up take him down.

"John, you don't have a choice," the colonel said softly. "You're being discharged."

Braun handed the envelope to Triton, who nearly refused to take it, as if it wouldn't be true if he didn't read it himself. But he did accept the orders, feeling the full impact of the pronouncement as his fingers touched the paper.

Colonel Braun stood tall, attempting to pay Triton the respect he deserved. "You served your country, your Corps, and your country with honor, son. Walk away with dignity."

But John Triton had never walked away from a challenge in his life. Not when he'd made the varsity football team his freshman year in high school. Not when he'd convinced Kate to marry him before he'd shipped out for the first time. He wasn't about to walk away from the service, no matter that the service didn't want him anymore.

"Damn it, Colonel," Triton said, trying to hold his anger in check. "I'm a Marine."

"One of the best, son," Braun said with a note of finality in his tone. "Remember that."

Triton's eyes met the colonel's with a mixture of defiance and confusion.

The colonel saluted. "On behalf of a grateful nation and the United States Marine Corps, I thank you for your loyal service."

Sergeant John Triton stood frozen, refusing to give up. Refusing to believe this was the end. He stood staring at his superior officer, knowing what was expected. He slowly, finally, raised his hand in salute. It was his last salute as a Marine. And it was done more out of defiance than respect.

5

"I'll take a cup of coffee," Rome ordered from the man at the coffee cart sitting on the sidewalk. The high-end cart sat right in the middle of the business district, where it catered to business people on the go who thought nothing of spending four dollars on something they could get for free in their break rooms.

"Just a coffee?" the proprietor of the fine establishment asked. "Nothing else?"

"Nope," Rome said, looking out on the street, past the small man. Though his attitude was casual, his mind was working overtime scoping out the area and making a mental list of all the salient details. This wasn't the first time he had been on this street, but he wanted to make sure he was aware of any changes in preparation for his return tomorrow.

"No shot of espresso? No nonfat, low-fat, part-skim milk?" the guy said with a laugh.

"Nada," Rome replied. "No caramel, vanilla, mocha, hazelnut crap either. Is that going to be a problem?"

"Problem?" the guy asked. "Probably be the easiest drink I've made all day. Just pour it in a cup and go."

"I may add some sugar," Rome conceded.

"Ah, a rebel," the man said, giving a pleased nod.

A man was walking toward him, carrying a small brown bag that looked as if his wife had packed him a school lunch that morning. Rome wondered if this was the target. It seemed likely. The guy was ultra-alert, with his eyes shifting all over the street as if he was waiting for an attack or something.

Rome immediately reconsidered his suspicion. The man was looking a little too obvious. He might have just as easily been lost and trying to find where he was going. Or it could have been his first time making such a large delivery, and he was paranoid about other people having an interest in the contents of his brown paper bag. It was kind of hard to tell as the man passed Rome and continued down the block.

Another man was coming from the opposite end of the street. He was particularly well dressed, carrying a briefcase, and heading straight for the jewelry store without a second glance to the sides. That could be the guy too. He did seem to have the air of a man with a mission.

This is exactly why Rome had set the plan for tomorrow. There were too many variables on the delivery. Not the least of which being that they didn't have an ID on the carrier. As it was, the guy with the paper bag kept walking, but the one with the briefcase actually went into the jewelry store. Not that that meant the one with the briefcase was the target either. He could have just been out buying something for his wife or mistress.

"Here you go," the vendor said to Rome as he handed over the steaming cup of plain old coffee. "Almost don't know what to charge for it," he added.

Rome handed over a fiver, and the guy made change. It was still less change than Rome would have expected if he had ordered the coffee at a diner, but money wasn't a big concern for Rome. It would be less of one in about twenty-four hours.

"You get much business here?" Rome asked the guy, taking his own eyes off the street for a bit. He dropped the loose change in the tip jar. There didn't seem much reason to tip the man for simply pouring a drink, but Rome hated jingling coins in his pockets. He didn't like to announce his movements that way.

"Can't complain," the vendor replied. "I'm only fillin' in, though. This is my brother's setup. He seems to be doin' okay."

Rome had already known the vendor wasn't the regular guy. That was the only reason he had approached the man in the first place.

"Your brother, he doesn't ever rent it out, does he?" Rome asked, taking a sip. He had to admit, it was pretty good coffee.

"Not that I know of," the vendor said, checking Rome out. He was dressed casually today, which meant a suit, but no tie. He knew he didn't look the type that would be inquiring about running a sidewalk vending cart, but people weren't always what they appeared.

Take the woman walking down the street right now. Classy. Stylish shoes that looked to be comfortable as well. A smart blue business suit with the blouse underneath opened just enough to be tempting, but still with a professional air. In her purse, she could be carrying millions of dollars worth of diamonds. Or she could be carrying nothing more than lipstick, car keys, and an empty wallet. You couldn't tell just by looking at her. She could be anything from an assistant to an executive.

And that was the point.

Diamond deliveries didn't come in armored cars with armed guards. Those kinds of deliveries were for banks and stores with large deposits. Places where it was obvious that money was being moved at some point. Maybe even the jewelry store did their banking that way. But not the diamonds. Those didn't arrive in some big show of security. That would be far too tempting a target. Losing the end-of-day receipts was nothing compared to a losing a shipment of diamonds.

No, the diamonds arrived discreetly; carried on an unidentified person's body. The person probably wasn't even carrying a weapon. This was how it was done in the diamond district of New York—where Rome's simple coffee would be twice the price of this one—and that's how it was done here in South Carolina.

When the woman kept walking past the diamond store, Rome crossed her off the list. There was probably nothing more valuable than a platinum credit card in her bag. Which was why today was just surveillance. He would wait until he had confirmation that the diamonds were on the premises. Once the delivery was made, store security would stand down a bit. That was the whole reason for having a vault on premises. Rome knew that everything was heightened on the day of a delivery of this magnitude. There were too many variables in making their assault today.

Who knew? Maybe the diamonds were already in the store.

"Your brother going to be here tomorrow?" Rome asked. "I'm looking to branch out a bit. This seems like a good location, but I've got several others in mind. Maybe he'd like to expand his operation?"

A mint-condition black '63 Ford Thunderbird convertible pulled up to the curb a few yards away, temporarily drowning out the vendor's response.

"I'm sorry," Rome said, glancing at the car. "Didn't quite catch that."

"I said, I doubt it," the vendor repeated. "My brother, he's not much for ambition. Though I guess he's got more than me, seein' how he's got his nice little business going here, and I just fill in on his off days."

"I see," Rome said, thinking. The stand was set up a nice distance from the jewelry store. Then again, it was mobile, so it could be moved to any position. Right now it was in front of the rare bookstore. The last time Rome had been in the area, he could have sworn it was over by the FedEx/Kinko's.

"Does your brother ever try other locations?" Rome asked. "May be better business across town."

"He hits the park some weekends," the vendor said. "But you'd have to ask him. He'll be here tomorrow. He's here every day during the week. Well, when I'm not fillin' in for him."

"I'll check it out," Rome said, having gotten the information he needed.

"Half-caf, caramel latte, no foam," the Thunderbird driver said as he approached the stand. The vendor shot a conspiratorial grin at Rome, who returned it as if they were old buddies. "And give me one of them chocolate croissants," he added.

"Nice ride." The vendor made conversation with his new customer as he whipped up the order.

The driver just nodded his appreciation, but didn't say anything.

"Good day for having the top down," Rome said to the driver. The sun was shining. The weather was warm enough that Rome could take his jacket off if he wanted. The forecast for tomorrow was just as nice, though they were calling for storms as the week wore on.

"Yeah," the driver said noncommittally.

"Get good mileage on that thing?" Rome asked.

"Careful now," the vendor warned the driver with a smile. "He might just offer to rent if from you. Open a business selling cars at this location."

"Well, now that you mention it," Rome said. "I have been in the market for a new car. Mind if I take a look?"

The driver shrugged as Rome finished off his coffee. He threw the cardboard cup in the trashcan beside the stand and moved over to the car. It was just the right amount of flash and substance. They didn't make cars like this anymore.

"So how fast can this thing go on the open road?" Rome asked as they walked away together.

"Fast as I want it to," the driver responded, taking a bite of the croissant and washing it down with a sip of his caffeine creation.

"I'm sure it does," Rome said, checking to confirm that they were out of earshot from the vendor. "So, Frank, is everything set for the pickup?"

"Yep," Frank replied through a mouthful of croissant.

"Not a man of many words," Rome said. "I like that." He especially liked it because he wouldn't be treated to another show of semi-chewed food.

"Delivery been made?" Frank asked after he finally swallowed.

"I think so," Rome said. It had probably been the guy with the briefcase. He was coming out of the store now, and it didn't look like he had bought anything while he was inside. "Can't tell for sure. If it was that easy, I could have taken the guy on the street myself."

"Instead of needing all the help you got lined up?"

"Exactly," Rome said. "I don't normally work with that many people. Don't like it, either. But I'm not entirely calling the shots on this one. We're following someone else's plan. I don't like that part at all."

"Which is where I come in," Frank concluded. "You

know, this deal isn't part of my usual trade. I prefer to stick with cars, not . . ."

Rome waited for Frank to finish the sentence, but the man just took another bite from the croissant. He was actually glad that Frank was smart enough to keep quiet about the second job he had been hired for. Never knew when someone was listening in.

"I have something for you," Frank said as he handed Rome a card.

"I thought you might," Rome said as he took it, silently reading the address written on it.

"The car will be waiting there for you tomorrow morning," Frank said.

"I'll be sending someone by," Rome said. "So, this car. I'm gonna like it, right?"

"Oh, yeah," Frank said, showing his first real sign of emotion. "You're gonna *love* it."

"Good," Rome said, starting to get excited. Before it had just been a plan to talk about, but now it was getting real. He felt like a kid on the eve of summer vacation. "I knew I could count on you."

Frank had a smug look of satisfaction on his face. "So—this other thing you had in mind?"

"Think you can handle it?" Rome asked.

"How big is the team?"

"Oh, there'll be about a half-dozen of us, give or take."

"Give or take?"

"Well, these things don't always go smoothly," Rome admitted, looking back down the street. It

46

wasn't too busy this afternoon, but one never knew how crowds could differ from day to day. All it took was one office to close early for some stupid reason and the entire area would be packed at the same time tomorrow.

"What exactly are we talking about?" the rider pressed.

Rome paused. Even though the coffee guy was a ways away, Rome wasn't comfortable speaking in specifics right out on the street. "How *does* one make this kind of request, exactly?"

"Well, let's talk about the dropoff," Frank said. "What kind of car are you looking for at the third point?"

"Nothing too flashy," Rome said. "You've already got us something to get out of town, but we need a vehicle that will get us a bit farther. I expect some people might be looking for us. Maybe automatic. My woman's pretty good with a stick, but better to keep it simple, if you ask me."

Frank nodded.

"Oh, and a two-seater would be perfectly fine," Rome added as if it were an afterthought.

6

Unfamiliar images drifted by the cab window. The city seemed like it had been another place when Triton had last been home. Even when stationed in the United States, he'd spent most of his time on the base. When he went home, it was to spend time alone with Kate. They rarely went out together, preferring to keep each other company rather than dealing with any distractions from their valuable time together.

So much had changed in the time he had been away. There were big things, like the huge Wal-Mart that had decimated the old Melrose Shopping Center. But Triton was much more interested in the subtle things, like new landscaping at the park and the movie theater that had expanded to a multiplex. Like the Wal-Mart, the movie theater must have been in development when Triton last shipped out, but he just never noticed it before. His life back then had been Kate and the Marines. Nothing else really mattered. Now he was going to have time to re-explore the area in which he grew up. Unsurprisingly, he wasn't exactly looking forward to it.

He was just thankful the cabbie didn't feel like talking about anything. The driver was simply content to listen to the radio playing an oldies station and keep his eyes on the road.

Kate could have picked him up at the airport. She had certainly wanted to meet him as soon as he got off the plane—or past security, as it was nowadays. (And once again, his mind went back to the fact that he was no longer working to make the country more secure.) But his flight had been delayed out of Dulles, and he'd told her that he'd just take a cab. Besides, she had studying to do.

She had her last final of the semester tomorrow. He was so impressed by her. To maintain their home, work a full-time job, and manage to put herself through medical school while he was gone was more than he could expect of anyone. Triton knew that he hadn't made it easier on her, considering what he did—what he had done—for a living. In between her work and studies, she had probably spent a fair amount of time worrying about him. At least that would stop. Now that he was coming home a failure.

No. He didn't want her to meet him at the airport.

His mind had flashed to all those homecomings he had seen on TV. A dozen people waiting with balloons and signs and American flags to celebrate the homecoming of the local hero. His parents were out of the picture, but he knew Kate would have been able to scrounge up a bunch of people to meet him. Then again, she knew him well enough to know that a welcoming committee was the last thing he would have wanted.

John Triton did not consider his homecoming a celebration. He didn't consider himself a hero. Real heroes didn't come slinking home in disgrace. They didn't come home to parades and adulation either. They just came home for a while, then went back out again, continuing to do what they were sworn to do. At least, that's how Triton looked at it. But he wouldn't be going back out anymore.

The cab pulled up in front of Triton's house. That was the one thing that hadn't changed since he left. Not that Kate would have had a lot of spare time to renovate or give the house a nice new paint job. But even if she had, it would still feel the same to Triton. Home was home no matter what. And he knew the woman waiting for him inside would be just the same as well.

Triton stepped out of the cab. Even out of uniform, he still had that buttoned-up feel. As if he would never be comfortable in his own skin. John reached into his pocket to get his keys, but he knew Kate well enough to know her trusting nature. The front door was unlocked. Besides, she was waiting for him.

He barely made it into the house before his beautiful wife was on him. Dressed in tight jeans and a somewhat revealing crop top, she ran up to Triton, screaming with joy and literally throwing herself into his arms. She wrapped her legs around him as he carried her through the house.

"John! Thank God you're home," she said, smiling with tears rolling down her cheeks as she kissed his lips and face and every piece of exposed flesh.

He noticed her textbooks spread out on the dining room table. She was hard at work again, just as he had suspected.

"Yeah, I'm home," John said with a mixture of sadness and joy. Though he hated the way he was being sent home, it was hard to be upset with Kate in his arms. It felt good to be with her. He never forgot how much he missed her when he was away, but now he remembered how nice it was to be with her. And he wanted to be with her in every way.

Triton carried her through the house, past her forgotten books, and into the master bedroom. They spilled onto the bed, tearing at each other's clothing. It had been too long since Triton had been with Kate in this way, with nothing but his dog tags between them.

He enjoyed the feel of her smooth skin beneath his callused hands. It had also been too long since he handled anything more delicate than an M67 fragmentation hand grenade. But this was far more pleasant an experience. And maybe just a little more dangerous as well.

For a time, Triton pushed the Marines out of his mind. He forgot about his problems. Forgot about his future. He stayed in the moment. With his wife. In their bed. It was the only place he wanted—no, *needed*—to be.

Two hours later Triton and Kate took a break from

their passion, retiring to the kitchen to share a pint of ice cream. Triton had forgotten how much he missed ice cream. Sure, they had some frozen yogurt concoction at the mess at Battalion Headquarters, but this was real honest-to-goodness ice cream with all the natural preservatives and artificial flavors he could ever want. And to be able to share it with his wife, who was sitting on the counter scantily dressed across from him, was almost more than Triton could wish for in a homecoming. Much better than balloons and welcome signs at the airport.

Kate scooped a spoonful of ice cream and fed it to Triton. A small drop of vanilla slid off the spoon and dribbled onto his chest, landing above his dog tags. He wasn't so sure that it was an accident, especially when Kate leaned in to lick it off. He could feel a stirring in his boxer shorts that two hours of passion hadn't yet fulfilled, but there was a deeper hunger inside him that needed to be quenched first.

Triton hadn't eaten since the plane from Germany to D.C. And that food wasn't even half the quality of the K-rations he lived off in the desert. He'd spent the connecting flight home too anxious to eat. That combined with two hours with his insatiable wife had left him with a hunger that ice cream alone could not handle. He knew Kate would have the fridge stocked with his favorites, so he started to move in that direction.

Kate stopped him by wrapping her legs around his waist and pulling him back to her. "No way. You're not going anywhere."

"I'm just gonna grab a—"

But the snack was forgotten as Kate interrupted him with a kiss. This one was different than the hours of passion they had just shared. Triton could feel this kiss held a deeper need. It was filled with more than enough emotion to keep Triton from walking away at that moment, or ever again.

Triton could see tears welling up in Kate's eyes as they finally broke apart.

"You all right?" he asked, not expecting the pure emotion of the moment.

"Yeah, I am now," she replied, forcing a smile. "I just can't believe that you're here . . . for good."

Triton still couldn't believe it either. Once they had left the bedroom, the thoughts and pain had flooded back into his brain. He was home. He would never be a Marine again. It was still hard getting his head around that concept. That he would never again wear the uniform. Never again fight for his country.

But at the same time, he was just realizing what it meant to Kate. He would never have to leave her again. Never have to worry her while he was off saving others. It was the first time he really saw how his life was affecting her. Triton planted a kiss on her forehead.

"You know what the hardest part about you leaving was?" she asked.

Triton didn't answer. He knew she needed to get it out. It had obviously been harbouring inside her for a long time. This was the first time he had ever come home for good. She would never have said any of this if she knew that he was going back out in a few months, as he previously would have. He was just there to listen to her for the moment and reassure her that everything was fine.

"It was the not knowing," she continued. "Not knowing where you were. Not knowing when or *if* you were coming home . . . Not knowing if I would get that phone call saying you wouldn't be."

Triton understood where she was coming from. He knew that it hurt her every time they said good-bye. But at the same time, it was his job. And he had been honest about that part of it from the start.

"You married a Marine, Kate," he gently reminded her.

"It was the uniform that got me," she said, dryly.

"I'm not wearing that uniform anymore." He had meant it to sound seductive. But the sentence came out loaded with a much different meaning.

"I know," she replied, catching on. "And I know that it's not going to be easy for you, John. But we'll figure it out together."

The look on her face was all Triton needed to know that he wasn't alone. As sure as she was happy about him being home, he knew that Kate also understood how much it was hurting him at the same time. And the best part was that neither one of them had to say it.

"I'm home now," Triton reassured her. "I'm not going anywhere." And this time, the sentence wasn't loaded. He meant it to sound the way that it did. He was happy to be with the woman he loved.

"Good," she said simply.

He managed to push aside his hunger for food, but he needed a beer. Reluctantly, he extracted himself from the tangle of Kate's legs and walked over to the refrigerator to grab a drink. "You want one?"

"No, thanks," Kate said.

Triton popped the top of the can. He could tell Kate wanted to say something. He could probably even guess what it was. But he didn't prod her to spit it out. He knew that he didn't necessarily want to hear what she would say.

Eventually, Kate got around to it, though. "Are you sure about starting this job tomorrow? I mean, there are so many other things you could do."

He didn't blame her for asking. The truth was, he wasn't sure. He couldn't see himself doing *anything* at the moment. But that was the biggest fear of all. He had already lost his sense of purpose. He couldn't lose his entire life.

"If I just sat here, I'd go insane," he told her, using the same logic he had on himself. "Joe pulled some strings for me, so I want to give it a shot."

Kate didn't seem to buy his answer. "Maybe if you just gave it a little while . . ."

"Kate, I gotta do this my way," he said a little forcefully. He caught himself and dialed it back a notch. "If I don't like it, I'll try something else."

"I just want you to be happy," Kate said, but he could tell that she was still unsure about his plan.

"I know," he said, throwing her a smile and hoping it would get one in return. It did, though he would have had to call it a reluctant smile at best.

"Okay, fine," she said, surrendering to him. However, he could tell in her eyes that she wasn't entirely giving in. "Tomorrow you go to work. But for the record, I think this is a bad idea."

It was a much smaller victory than he was used to, but he would take it. He didn't know if he could go on if Kate didn't support him. Honestly, he wasn't too keen on the idea either. But it beat sitting around the house wallowing in self-pity while Kate was at school studying to become a doctor.

John Triton had never sat still a day in his life, and he wasn't about to start now. Besides, who knew? Security could open up a whole new list of possibilities for Triton. He could go into personal security or even become a private investigator. But right now he couldn't focus on anything too far down the road. He still wondered if there was a way he could get back into the Marines. Some back door he could use, or maybe an old friend of his father's with the right connections. He would never go to his father directly, since that door had closed long ago. The job that Joe had arranged for him would have to be enough until he could figure out what to do with the rest of his life.

"And, hey," she continued with a look in her eye that Triton had seen not two hours earlier. "After work, you can come home and play."

"Why wait until then?" Triton asked as he put down his beer and went back into her embrace. This time, they didn't make it out of the kitchen.

7

The Mercedes eased to a stop along the curb on Roosevelt Boulevard beside an African-American man in his twenties drinking cappuccino at the coffee cart. Rome's new friend wasn't manning the cart. Instead there was an equally short man with similarly dark hair and a slightly bronzed skin tone. Rome figured it was the cart's owner, the brother to the guy he had met the day before.

Otherwise, the scene wasn't much different. Maybe the coffee cart was a few feet farther down the street than it had been the day before. But basically it was in the same location. A few people milled about on the street, but it looked like business was slow at the moment. Otherwise, it was a quiet afternoon.

Rome didn't think it would be that way for long.

He looked out the right-hand window. Traditionally, he'd have to be the passenger to do this, but this was an SL 600 series Mercedes with right-hand drive. He might not be the one driving it away, but there was no chance he wasn't going to take the opportunity to test it out driving there.

When the car had rolled up this morning, Rome

wasn't exactly pleased to see what Frank had sent him. A car like this wasn't exactly inconspicuous. Once Rome got over the initial concern, he was able to see just how well it would work for his plan. The car was an extravagance, but for his plan to work, he wanted to make his entrance while looking the part of the upscale shopper.

Besides, it was just so darned fun to drive.

Rome looked out at the man drinking his cappuccino. He didn't seem to have a care in the world, sitting there at a little side table, his canvas bag at his feet. The man's style seemed smooth and unruffled. Of course, you couldn't tell that much about a man just by looking at him through a car window. He could turn out to be a mass-murdering lunatic. One never knew what a person would be capable of, especially if there was a double shot of espresso in his drink. Rome wondered how many caffeine-fueled rages had landed people in jail since the coffee explosion of the nineties.

The coffee cart was three doors down from the small "old money" jewelry store. Rome had been right about it moving. It had been four doors down yesterday. It didn't make much difference, though. The plan was specific, but not that precise.

Sitting in the car in the left-side passenger seat was a man dressed just as nicely as Rome. His name was Vescera. The men weren't exactly friends, but Rome had worked with him before and knew he was good enough to get the job done.

The guy had this wry acerbic wit that, to be honest,

Rome never found all that funny. But he wasn't along for the laughs. Vescera tended to be cool as ice in most situations. They had never before worked together on a score as large as this one had the potential to be. When this kind of money was involved, you really got to see what made people tick.

"I'll be right back," Rome said as he unbuckled his seat belt.

" 'You got it, man,' " Vescera replied with a false accent that sounded a bit forced. It stopped Rome in his tracks, his hand resting on the door handle.

"What?"

" 'You got it, man,' " Vescera said again with an even thicker accent. "You know, *Scarface*."

"Do it again?" Rome asked, considering.

Vescera sat up a little straighter, like he was performing for Rome. " 'You got it, man.' "

"Wow," Rome said, opening the car door, "that's horrible."

Rome got out of the car without glancing back. He didn't mind having a bit of fun on the job, but there was nothing the least bit entertaining about Vescera's impression. And what's the point in that?

The guy working at the coffee cart smiled at Rome. For a moment, he thought the guy's brother had given a detailed description of Rome in case he came back with more questions about the business. But Rome was just being paranoid. The man probably smiled at every passerby, hoping they'd stop off to buy something from him.

Without a second glance at the cart, Rome continued for the jewelry store. The name in the window read "Titizian's—Diamond Traders Est. 1926." He opened the glass door and let himself in. If this had been a larger city, a doorman would have opened the door for him. Security would have been in force in the place. But this was not a larger city. Everything here was on a smaller scale—except for the delivery that had come in the day before.

The selling floor was busy with moneyed clients sitting at ornate tables for private showings of jewels. At one table, a young couple was shopping for engagement rings. Rome could tell by the looks on their faces that the girl had much more expensive taste than the guy could afford. The young man even had a small trickle of sweat sliding down his forehead. Rome gave the marriage a couple years. Just long enough for them to be on their second kid when the husband decides he's had enough and can't take another day of her greedy ways and keep-up-with-the-Joneses mindset.

At another table, there was an older woman who obviously had enough jewelry and enough money to buy plenty more. Maybe this was her way of punishing her husband for cheating on her. Or maybe it was her way to treat herself with her well-earned bonus check.

Either way, she wasn't stupid enough to wear the real jewelry out and about in the daytime. Her neck, ears, arms, and fingers were adorned with fakes. Rome didn't have to know anything about jewelry to be able to tell that. He knew about human nature. The real stuff was safely in the vault at home in the back of her closet, waiting for a night out on the town along with the new friends she was buying today.

Another man in his thirties was standing at a counter, flirting with the sexy female clerk who was helping him with watches. From where Rome stood, he could tell that the guy was trying on a nice gold watch that probably cost more than the young husband-to-be was willing to spend on his future bride.

The rest of the small store was filled with assorted staff and browsers, probably just in to dream, but not actually buy anything. And, of course, there was Mr. Titizian; the second man with that particular moniker to stand in the store since its opening eighty years earlier. Rome wondered if the old guy had any sons to carry on the business after he was gone. He also hoped that the man wasn't about to do anything that would force Rome to create a situation wherein the old man's sons had to take over the place tomorrow.

Rome gave a nod to the beauty helping the guy out with his watch purchase and continued into the store. He walked up to a man wearing a simple business suit and, without blinking, decked the man with a jaw-breaking roundhouse right.

The businessman dropped to the floor. Before anyone else could register what had happened, Rome reached into the fallen man's jacket, past the cheap metal "Security" badge pinned on the vest underneath, and pulled the man's gun.

Rome stuck the guard's gun into his own waistband as he turned to face the customers. Panic began to ripple through the store as the clerks and shoppers realized what was going on. The young fiancé grabbed for his intended and threw himself in front of her, causing Rome to rethink his earlier estimate of the length of their future union. The wealthy woman looked as if she was about to have a heart attack, clutching her heart and her fake jewels.

As for the man buying the watch—he simply smiled his flirtatious smile at the panicking saleswoman. He didn't seem at all fazed by the sudden shift in the afternoon of shopping. But there was a good reason for that.

"Excuse me," the man said, stepping away from the saleswoman. Rome noticed that he still had the expensive watch on his wrist.

The man, whose name was Bennett, drew two guns from his jacket while Rome drew his own piece. Their eyes met for a moment before continuing on to scan the store around them. Both Bennett and Rome kept their guns moving, covering everyone in the room. Neither of the men wavered in their cool demeanor.

"Everybody down!" Rome shouted in as calm a manner as he could while still getting across the fact that he meant business. No need to panic the people any further and set any of them off to try being a hero.

"Move!" Bennett added loudly, negating any calming effect Rome had been going for with his tone.

But still, it worked. Clerks and shoppers fell to the

ground, many of them praying to whatever God they believed in. Rome found that part unnecessary. If everyone did as they were told, they'd get out of there safely. No need for tears and false promises to the powers-that-be.

Probably.

"Ladies and gentlemen," Rome addressed the group, "keep your heads down and your mouths shut. I don't want to see *any* eye contact. I have severe intimacy issues and a gun, so do yourselves a favor and don't look up."

As expected, Rome looked to the back counter and saw that a man in his late seventies was still standing. The second Titizian, who had been a diamond man for over fifty years, was behind the counter looking panicked and confused. Rome could tell the man was silently calculating the stock and hoping that the robbers didn't know about the good stuff in the back.

Too bad for Titizian, but that was exactly what Rome had in mind. He flashed the man a smile that did not put Titizian even remotely at ease.

Sure, the store probably had had several smash-and-grab robberies since it opened its doors in 1926. Even a couple armed bandits might have come knocking in the thirties and forties, back when that kind of thing happened regularly. But this probably was the first time he had ever witnessed such a brazen attack in the middle of the day, as far as Rome could tell. And it was clear that Daddy had never prepared the guy for a day like this.

"You!" Rome said to Titizian, who was paralyzed with fear and indecision. "There's one under the counter and another alarm by your left foot. You go for either one of 'em, I'll show everybody here what the inside of your brain looks like."

Rome had reached the glass security door at the back of the shop. A young kid, barely older than twenty, was practically quaking behind the glass. The kid really didn't need to look so scared. He was probably the safest person in the room.

Or not.

"What I want is on the other side of the door," Rome said, eyeing the clerks, expecting that none of them had any intention of playing the hero. "But that's going to be a little tricky because"—he fired twice at the glass—"it's bulletproof."

The bullets bounced harmlessly off the glass, but the kid locked inside the room had still ducked out of the way out of pure survival instinct. He was slowly rising to his feet, almost surprised that he was still alive in spite of knowing that nothing could have gotten to him in there.

"So here's what we do," Rome said as he lifted an attractive woman off the floor. She let out a short squeal as he held her to him. "Hi, honey. Can I borrow you for a second?"

He didn't wait for an answer as he pushed her toward the door, past the horrified storeowner, and right up to the glass. Only that glass and a couple inches separated her face from the guy inside the vault.

"How you doin', sport?" he asked the kid behind the glass. His tone was polite and nonthreatening, as if he wasn't ready to kill everyone in the room. From where he stood, he could see the kid's nametag. It read "Chris."

"I know you can hear me in there, Chris," Rome continued, tapping on the glass. "We're gonna do this real simple. I count to three, if the door's not open, she's history." He held the gun up to the woman's side threateningly. "And then, one by one, so is everyone else."

Mr. Titizian looked horrified, like he was about to wet his Depends undergarments.

The kid behind the glass was frozen on the other side of the door. His hand reached for the keypad while he looked to his boss for guidance. Rome followed Chris's eyes to Titizian. The older man clearly didn't know what to do. All he managed was to shake his head, but it certainly wasn't clear to Rome what the man meant by it. It could have meant, "Don't open the door," or just as easily been indicating, "I don't know what to do."

Rome doubted that Chris would understand the meaning either.

"Now I know the whole 'counting to three' thing is a bit of a cliché," Rome admitted, enjoying himself, "but it's just so cool. So here we go."

Rome raised the gun to the woman's temple.

"One . . ."

Chris looked back to Titizian. His hand slid away from the keypad.

"Don't look at him. He can't help you."

The woman was struggling against Rome and crying. Her hands were only inches from the security guard's gun, still stuck in Rome's waistband.

"Two . . ."

Rome pulled hard at the woman's hair as she pleaded for her life. "God, please. I have children." She had directed her cries to the kid behind the glass. Even though he did not have the gun, he was the one with her life in his hands.

"I don't think he cares," Rome said, never taking his eyes off Chris.

Refusing to let her death be on his hands, Chris made the hasty decision and reached for the keypad again. Quivering, he tapped a code into the panel next to the security door. As the security door slowly slid open, the woman grabbed for the gun in Rome's waistband and pulled it free.

Titizian let out a small cry of relief.

The woman backed away from Rome, but instead of turning the gun on him, she turned it on Titizian. The man's relief quickly turned back to shock. In the meantime, Rome rushed through the security door.

"You're having a very bad day," the woman, Angela, said to the storeowner.

Inside the diamond vault, Rome threw a custom-made velvet pouch onto the counter.

"Fill it," he told the kid.

Chris pulled a metal box out of the inner vault, while Rome moved to a security panel on the side wall.

Pressing a button, he popped the disk out of the wall-mounted digital recorder and pocketed it. Once the visual evidence of the crime was safely in his possession, Rome turned his attention back to Chris.

The kid was filling the pouch with the most perfect VSI diamonds that Rome's untrained eye had ever seen.

Outside the jewelry store, the afternoon was calm and serene. There was no sign that anything abnormal was going on inside. Vescera had thought he heard a couple shots fired earlier, but that was only because he was listening intently for any sign of trouble. No one else on the street would have noticed. Certainly the guy manning the coffee cart hadn't even flinched. The black guy, however, seemed to notice the noise too. But he didn't really react either.

Vescera had slid over to the driver's side in preparation for the getaway. He was looking forward to getting the car out on the open road. Rome wouldn't even let him drive to the store. He couldn't blame the guy, though. It was a sweet ride.

He wanted to listen to the radio while he waited, but that would have negated his whole purpose for being there in the first place. Still, he wished he could have something to do while he passed the time. Everyone else on the crew was having fun at the moment.

Sirens in the distance brought him out of his thoughts. Someone inside must have tripped an alarm. Either that, or maybe someone noticed the shots from one of the adjacent buildings. Either way, trouble was coming. It wasn't close yet, but it was definitely on its way.

Viscera picked up the radio and pressed the transmit button. "We gotta move," he said calmly into the mike.

Rome heard Vescera's warning through his earpiece. He could tell there was still time by the tone in the man's voice. They were almost done inside. The kid had just finished loading up the pouch, and Rome had confirmed there was no other surveillance equipment.

"*Guys,*" Vescera said over the comm with slightly more urgency in his tone. "*The police are coming.*"

Rome grabbed the pouch and made for the vault exit.

"Rome, you gotta hit me," Chris said in an excited whisper from behind him.

Rome froze.

Everything had been going so well.

He slipped the pouch into his jacket pocket and slowly turned toward Chris, wishing that the kid hadn't said his name. Wishing that he hadn't forced him into this situation.

"I don't know," Chris stupidly continued, keeping his voice low, but not low enough for Rome. "Just knock me out or something. It's got to look real."

Rome coolly raised his gun and shot Chris in the head. A chorus of stifled cries came from the showroom as the kid's lifeless body crumpled to the floor. *Yeah, that looks real enough.*

"Thank you all for a lovely, and profitable, after-noon," Rome said as he moved out to the sales floor, where Angela and Bennett continued to keep everyone down. He could see the look of surprise on Angela's face, but Bennett didn't even flinch. They could all hear the sirens approaching.

"As you can hear," Rome continued, "the police are on their way. For your own safety, I suggest you all re-main inside until we're gone. Maybe finish up your shopping."

Rome picked a watch off the counter. It was from the selection that Bennett had been looking at earlier. The watch was silver with a black face. It had diamond chips for numbers with a larger diamond at the twelve spot. He slipped it onto his wrist and led Angela and Bennett out of the store.

The trio charged out into the street, heading past the coffee cart for the Mercedes. As Angela and Ben-nett piled inside, a police cruiser came screeching around the corner, making a wild turn onto the street.

Rome popped the trunk with an electric key and pulled an M16 A2 from the car. He stepped out into the street. As the police car raced toward him, Rome raised the gun and sprayed the cruiser with bullets.

As the bullet-riddled cop car skidded to a halt, the African-American man at the coffee cart suddenly went into action as the vendor dove to the ground. The man—Morgan—ripped an Armburst antitank weapon out of the canvas bag at his feet. He shouldered the miniature cannon and fired a shot directly into the hood of the police car.

The squad car, hit hard, blew straight up into the air.

None of this had been part of the plan, but Rome was relishing every minute of it. He watched as Morgan took the weapon off his shoulder, dropped a buck in the coffee guy's tip jar, and joined Rome at the car.

"Subtle," Rome commented to Morgan, making the king of all understatements as they got into the car.

Vescera pulled the Mercedes away as they drove past the flaming cop car.

No one spoke as they continued through the downtown streets. Additional sirens were racing toward them. Rome was angry that someone had managed to sound the alarm. Then, of course, there was that kid, Chris, using his name. The plan hadn't gone down perfectly—for instance, blowing up the cop car had been entirely unexpected—but it was over. He had millions of dollars of diamonds sitting in his jacket, right next to his heart.

After several careful turns while Vescera did his best not to call attention to their car, he pulled into a public parking structure and parked. They would wipe the car down and abandon it there before heading out for an innocent night on the town to celebrate.

8

"Don't worry," Detective Van Buren said into the phone. "I'm good for it. Now, if you don't mind, I'm at work right now and don't have time for this." He slammed the phone down in the cradle.

"Problem, Van?" his friend Detective Charlie Bryant asked as he got off his own call.

"Nothing I can't handle," Van Buren replied. It was bad enough that people would bother him at home, but it was downright annoying when they started calling at work. "What you got going on?"

"Heist down on Roosevelt," Charlie replied. "Report of shots fired. Squad cars en route. It sounds like something big. Definitely something that's going to take up the rest of the day. And Jen was hoping I'd come home early for a change." He seemed to put some none-too-subtle emphasis on that last part.

Van Buren looked at his watch. It was still early in the afternoon, but he knew these kinds of things could stretch on for hours. And Charlie's wife had been harping on him for weeks about his ability to stay later than necessary at crime scenes.

"Let me take it," Van Buren said, as if it was the

biggest imposition in the world. Honestly, he was looking to get out of the office about now anyway. But he didn't need Charlie knowing that. "You go home to the missus on time for once."

"You sure?" Charlie asked.

"Yeah," Van Buren replied, getting up from his chair. "Just bring me leftovers tomorrow."

Suddenly there was a flurry of activity in the squad room. Officers everywhere were slamming down phones, making new calls, and hurrying out of the room.

"What's up?" Van Buren asked, grabbing the nearest officer.

"That diamond store heist," Officer Dawes replied. "We got a report of an officer down. Some kind of explosion or something."

Van Buren's blood ran cold. He shot a look to Charlie.

"You want me to come along?" Charlie asked.

"I'll call you if I need help," Van Buren answered, checking his gun. The last thing he had expected to deal with today was the death of an officer. The case had automatically gone from something of interest to something of high priority. He knew that he should bring Charlie along, but Van Buren wanted to keep it simple. The more detectives on scene, the more complicated his job became.

He almost made a joke about expecting Charlie to bring in a full meal for him tomorrow, but stopped himself. It was no longer a joking matter.

73

It only took a few minutes for Van Buren to wind his way through the downtown streets with lights flashing on his unmarked car. The streets were already backing up as officers cordoned off the area. It would be hell come rush hour when everyone was trying to get home.

Van Buren knew he was only making it worse as he kept in contact with the station over the radio. But he needed to make sure the right roads were closed and the escape routes were covered. There was no room for anyone to screw up on this. Once a police officer has lost his life, the force will be out for blood. Van Buren needed to know that he was in control.

He arrived at the scene to find the police car still smoldering. Firefighters had managed to put most of the fire out. As Van Buren got out of his car, he could see a charred body inside. He must have known the officer. The department wasn't that large. He braced himself for the information as the first officer on scene approached.

"Detective," Officer McKinnon said as he reached Van Buren.

"Who is it?" Van Buren asked.

"It's Stein," McKinnon replied. "Poor guy didn't have a chance. Witnesses say it was some guy with a bazooka."

Van Buren tried to hide his shock. You didn't run into guys with bazookas every day on the street. Not in South Carolina. Seemed a bit excessive for a robbery. Rage welled up deep within him as he took in the scene. He hadn't spoken with anyone yet, but he already knew there was no reason for this level of violence. No reason at all.

"Witnesses?" the detective asked.

"Several customers and staff in the store," McKinnon reported, "and a coffee guy out on the street."

"I'll talk to the coffee guy first, then take in the scene and interview the witnesses inside. Starting with the security guard," Van Buren said.

The detective started on the street, interviewing the guy that owned the coffee cart: Mr. Martinez. The witness filled him in on the black man with the bazooka, although Van Buren was pretty sure it was technically a grenade launcher. Then again, the two weapons could have been the same thing. It wasn't like the coffee merchant was up on his heavy artillery. He couldn't help but think that the idiots involved in the heist had used dynamite to swat a fly.

After Martinez had given him a vague description of the people involved, Van Buren went into the jewelry store to checked out the crime scene. He took preliminary statements from each of the witnesses and found that there was enough contradictory information from each of them to make it difficult to ID the bad guys. Once that was done, he thoroughly examined the scene, taking in what the witnesses had told him and combining it with the clues the space itself had provided.

With all that information at hand, he filtered out the stuff he deemed unnecessary and came up with what the rest of the team needed to hear. The witnesses were taken outside while he met with the on site team to detail the crime.

Detective Van Buren stood among the police officers and CSIs in the diamond store, surveying the scene one last time before he spoke. He maintained a professional calm that came only from years of experience. He was good at his job, and he loved doing it. But today, he felt the tension of his work weigh on his shoulders more than usual as he walked everyone through the particularly brazen robbery.

"All right, here's what we know," he said, pausing for a moment to make sure he had everyone's attention. "There were five of them. Three inside, two waiting outside."

Van Buren moved around the shop, mimicking Rome's movements from hardly an hour earlier. It was his ritual, re-creating a crime with what he knew to be startling accuracy. This was part of the show that made him the most talked-about detective in the precinct house.

"Number One dropped the guard here," he said, indicated where Rome had knocked the guy to the floor. "He and Number Two pull guns. 'Everybody down, blah, blah, blah.' They want what's in the vault, but how do they get in? Take a hostage. Threaten to kill her. Magically the vault door opens." He moved over to the still open vault. "They're in. But, look out. Surprise, surprise, our hostage—she's with the bad guys."

That much they knew from the witness reports. Though the witnesses were still sketchy on physical descriptions from the shock that they were still in, they had all pretty much recounted the same story. This is where Van Buren came in and earned his pathetic excuse for a paycheck.

"Now once they get in here," Van Buren continued from the doorway to the vault, "they don't bother with the small stuff. They go right for the vault with twelve million in diamonds in it. Ironically, the same diamonds that were delivered just twenty-four hours ago." He moved over to one of the CSIs. "What are the odds? How did our guys know they'd be so lucky today?"

Van Buren looked back to the body in the vault. Christopher Grunlip. Age: twenty-two. *Won't be seeing twenty-three.* "We could ask our friend on the floor over here. I'll bet he knows."

Van Buren moved out of the vault and continued to the front of the store.

"Then they make their way outside, where they have a car and two friends waiting." He moved over to the store window, and the team followed. "Everything is perfect until they hear sirens. That's when Johnny Armani goes full tilt—opening fire until his African-American friend can back him up with an RPG. Boom. That's all . . . done. Good-bye."

He ended his speech with a glance at the burned-out shell of the police car a few yards away from the store. He took a momentary pause out of respect for the fallen Officer Stein. The officers in the room with him bowed their heads as well. When he turned back to the investigating team, he was glad to see they were giving him their undivided attention, as he had expected.

"If these guys have any brains at all," he said in conclusion, "they're on their way out of town."

"They were smart enough to pull this off," a young cop Van Buren didn't know all that well chimed in.

"They killed a cop," Van Buren said with barely contained anger. "How smart could they be?"

Nods of agreement filled the room.

"What's the status on the roadblocks?" Van Buren asked.

"All major streets leading out of downtown are blocked, rotating patrols on the smaller streets," McKinnon reported. "Highway patrol has the major arteries out of the city covered."

"Okay," Van Buren said. "We'll cover them through the night. If we don't have them by then, I expect they'll be long gone."

9

Triton tried not to look at the clock. He kept his focus on the people rushing about the lobby as he sat behind the oversize security desk in a uniform that was two sizes too small. He wasn't big on metaphors or stuff like that, but his twelfth-grade English teacher, Mrs. Cooper, would have loved this scene. Everyone around him moving in different directions while he was stuck behind a security desk.

And it was only his first day.

It wasn't that Triton had any problem sitting motionless in a confined space. He had once spent almost twenty-four hours in a spider hole in Tikrit waiting for an insurgent leader to come out of hiding and into the open. Back then, he'd kept his mind on the mission to occupy the time. He hadn't looked at his watch once.

But here, in the lobby of the Marathon Building, he didn't have a mission to keep his mind focused on. He didn't even have a future to think about. All he had was his buddy Joe reading a magazine beside him.

Triton thought that his skills of observation might come in handy in the job. And maybe they would eventually. But so far, it was pretty obvious who was going to make trouble for security and who was just going to go about their day not even acknowledging Triton's existence.

Take, for example, the piece of work that just entered the building. He was wearing a flashy expensive suit that proved that just because someone has money doesn't mean he has good taste. He was talking way too loudly on his cell phone, not caring that he was bothering the people around him. All in all, he had that money attitude that people have when they have some cash, but not nearly enough to get away with the act.

The dark-haired man came in flanked by his two buddies. Triton had seen their type before. They were the kind of "friends" that were only interested in the guy for what money he did have. All three of them were probably coked out of their minds, laughing way too loudly at their own private jokes. In the middle of the day, no less.

The two pals couldn't have been more of a contradiction. One was a clean-cut pretty boy. Obviously he was the one that brought the ladies to the trio. The other guy was clearly the muscle. Bald with a goatee and earring, he looked a bit like a cartoon genie. So Alpha Dork had one guy to score him women and another to keep him safe. Maybe he had more money than his expensive cheap suit had led Triton to believe.

The two goons split off to the magazine stand while their leader waited for an elevator.

Triton expected trouble from these guys. Not the

kind of *real* trouble he was used to dealing with. Nothing, say, on the level of a Pashtun warlord on some kind of mission of martyrdom. That wasn't Triton's world anymore. No, this would be trouble of the annoying kind. He could already see it coming.

Triton looked over at Joe, but his friend was far too absorbed in his own dilemma to notice the potential problem.

"What if I got a Soloflex?" Joe asked, looking down past the magazine to his pudgy stomach. "No, no, no . . . *Bow*flex. Nah, Soloflex . . . How long till I look like you?"

"You gonna be disciplined?" Triton asked as he watched the tool get on the elevator while his thuggy friends remained behind.

"Yeah!"

"Gonna train hard?"

"No question!"

"Diet?"

"You know it!"

Triton gave his friend the once-over. Joe had certainly let himself go a bit since their high school days on the football field. "Never."

"That's not cool, because I'm sensitive and you know it," Joe said, but he was looking hurt in an overly forced and melodramatic way that implied he knew that Triton spoke the truth.

Triton gave his friend a smirk as he looked out over the lobby. He could already tell that nothing really happened there on a daily basis. Even the tool's friends weren't all that interesting. One was reading *GQ*, with the other was perusing *Men's Fitness*. Triton suspected that both men were just looking at the pictures.

"Is that all you do all day?" Triton asked. Joe's head was still in his own fitness magazine. He, at least, seemed to be reading the thing. Then again, he probably worked his way through one entire magazine a day, at the very least.

"I had a GameBoy, but they took it," Joe replied. He seemed to notice Triton's lack of interest. "C'mon, man, this is a great job. Good money . . . benefits . . . couple—two, three years—they move you into management."

Triton thought about what his friend was saying and did the math. "How long you been working for this company?"

"Nine years."

"How come you're not in management?" Triton asked, trying not to be insulting with the implication. Not that he thought Joe would be offended.

"Politics," was Joe's simple reply. But with Joe these things rarely stopped at simple. "For some reason they think that every time you get suspended, you should start over again."

Triton wasn't sure if Joe was joking or not, but he chose to let the comment pass. He did wonder what Joe could have done that would get him suspended. There didn't seem anything all that interesting to do that would get him in trouble. But Triton didn't say that either. He didn't want to come off as ungrateful.

Joe had pulled some strings to get Triton the job. At least, that's what he had said. Seems to Triton all Joe had to do was say he had a friend that just got out of the Marines, and Triton would have been in. Their boss had barely asked him any questions on the phone interview while Triton was still in Germany. The guy didn't even want to know why Triton was leaving the Marines. And Triton hadn't volunteered the information.

Triton focused his attention back on the people milling about the huge lobby, while trying very hard to stay away. That was when he saw someone heading directly to the security desk. This wasn't the first time. People tended to treat it like it was an information booth, asking where such-and-such's office was located. But this time it was different. The person didn't look confused and wandering. He was making a beeline straight for the desk.

Then Triton finally recognized the guy. He wasn't surprised it took a second. The kid had shot up about a foot and filled out since the last time Triton had seen the puny little runt. It was Brian McCray, the teenage son of Triton's (and Joe's) high school football coach. Triton had known the kid since he was just a little squirt.

"Whoa! John Triton!" Brian said as he reached the desk.

"Brian!" Triton replied. It had been years since he'd seen the kid. "What's up, brother?"

"How you been, man? You workin' here?" Brian

asked. Triton couldn't help but think there was a slight tone of disbelief and maybe some disappointment in that question. Or maybe Triton was projecting his own thoughts onto the kid.

"Yeah," Triton said, trying to sound enthused. "Joe hooked me up."

"His jersey still hangs in our gym," Brian said proudly to Joe.

"That's cool, man," Joe replied. "Where's my jersey hangin'?"

"I don't know, dude," Brian replied, playfully. "Your closet?"

"Good times," Joe said sarcastically.

"How's your old man?" Triton asked the kid.

"Retiring from the team," Brian said. He took a moment to take in the surroundings. Even a teenager saw the dead-end aspect of the job. "We got word out for a new coach."

Triton considered it for a moment. It would be better than sitting on his butt all day. But it just reminded him of why he didn't take the opportunity in the first place. "I had a shot at humpin' you guys down the field years ago, but I joined up instead."

"That's you all the way, man," Brian said, showing him the kind of respect most teens just didn't give. "But you're back now, so check it out."

The desk phone rang, and Joe answered it. "Security."

Brian held up the package he was holding. "I gotta drop this off. It's great seeing you, John!"

"Tell your dad I said hello," Triton replied as he watched the kid race off to the open elevator.

"Will do!" Brian yelled back as the elevator doors closed.

Triton looked over at Joe as he hung up the phone.

"Psycho ex-boyfriend on twelve," Joe said.

Triton shot a glance over at the two goons by the magazine stand; the overly manicured one and his buddy, the genie. Somehow he suspected this had something to do with their friend.

The two guards moved out from behind the desk and crossed to the elevator.

"Looking forward to seeing a little action?" Joe asked as he pressed the up button.

Triton chose not to respond. He couldn't imagine just how *little* action the pipsqueak upstairs would provide.

"I gotcha," Joe said, playfully. "You're getting into the zone. Did the same thing on the football field, you did. That killer instinct. Must have come in handy overseas. Get your enemy in your sights and wait. Just wait him out, all silent. Just sitting there, thinking about all the things you're gonna—"

"Joe."

"Yeah."

"Knock it off."

"Gotcha," Joe said as he clamped his mouth shut.

The elevators opened, and they stepped inside. An older woman came up and was about to step in with them, but Triton held out his hand to stop her. "Sorry, ma'am. Emergency." He assumed that it wasn't a real emergency, but if it was, then they couldn't risk being slowed by stopping on every floor.

"Fine," the woman said, but looked fairly peeved at the same time.

And that was the issue right there. Sergeant John Triton had led men in battle. He had saved countless lives on the field. He had made a difference. And now, Security Guard John Triton was stopping little old ladies from using the elevator so he could deal with some coked-up, entitled wannabe pretty boy.

It wasn't that Triton thought the job was beneath him. The guards at his father's building had always been cool to him growing up. There were certainly less respectable jobs that he could have been stuck in. He wasn't some dilettante who thought he deserved better than his best friend beside him. But, much like his current uniform, building security just wasn't the right fit.

"When we get up there, let me take the lead," Joe said. "I've dealt with these situations before. You tend to get screwed-up personal problems more than anything around here. Disgruntled employees needing to be escorted from the building. Maybe a few domestic disturbances that spill over to the workplace. Nothing too exciting, like corporate espionage or anything."

Triton found it hard to believe corporate *anything* would be all that exciting, truth be told. People screwing each other over because of some numbers on spreadsheets was nothing compared to watching people live and die for their beliefs, messed up as some of those beliefs may have been.

The elevator opened on the twelfth floor, depositing the guards into the swank lobby of a high-end law firm. It was the kind of place that only handled million-dollar clients and had shiny chrome espresso machines instead of plastic coffeemakers. It was the kind of office in which Triton's own father had worked.

It was the kind of place Triton knew he'd never fit in either.

"Excuse me," Joe said as they stepped up to the comely receptionist. "We got a call about—"

"Rick, have you lost your mind?" a woman's voice was straining not to yell from down the hall. "This is my job."

Triton didn't bother wait for Joe to follow as he turned toward the noise.

"Never mind," he heard Joe say. "I think we can find our way."

"Like I give a shit!" the guy, Rick, said much louder than was necessary. "Where is he?"

Triton passed several heads popping out of office doors and up from their cubicles. Joe had caught up, and the two were heading for the cause of the disturbance together. Triton wasn't surprised in the least to see that the putz who'd left his two friends downstairs was the one making all the racket.

"Weekend conference!" Rick screeched in an unmanly voice. "You were with him! That's why you didn't answer your cell all weekend."

Triton and Joe had reached the couple. She was an attractive dark-haired woman with a strong presence, obviously trying hard not to lose it in the middle of the office. It made no sense that she would be with such a loser, but Triton had seen stranger things in his life.

Since this was only his first day, Triton let Joe step up and take the lead. Joe seemed to stand a little taller than he normally did, giving himself more of a professional air than Triton had previously thought possible.

If this were the desert, Triton would know how to handle a moron like this. But in the shiny glass corporate offices, he suspected a quick punch to the face wouldn't go over so well.

"Sir, could you please come with us?" Joe asked formally. As much as he seemed to be unfit for the job, Triton couldn't help but think his friend was in his element at the moment.

"Don't mess with me, pork chop," Rick said, barely pausing to glare.

Joe wordlessly mouthed the words "Pork chop?" at Triton before looking down at his body.

"Rick, you're causing a scene," the woman said through clenched teeth.

"You think this is causing a scene?" Rick asked. "Wait till I tell Daddy about the little whore he raised."

"Sir," John said, slipping past Joe. It was one thing to cause a scene, it was another thing entirely to speak to a woman that way. "I'm going to have to ask you—"

88

"Ask me to what?" Rick said, spinning on Triton. The fact that there was a difference in height, weight, and pure muscle between the two of them didn't seem to faze the guy in the least. "Have a seat, flat-top. I'll get to you in a second."

Joe shot Triton a look that basically said, "Are you gonna take that?"

Of course, the answer was no.

Triton grabbed the idiot by the back of the neck and yanked him off his feet. It would have only taken a shift of the wrist to snap the guy's neck, but that would definitely qualify as excessive force in this case. Instead, Triton dragged the guy down the hall, literally kicking and screaming all the way to the elevator.

"Get your hands off me," Rick cried. "Do you know who I am?"

"The guy who can't get it up!" his *ex*-girlfriend called out behind them, once again proving the adage: never mess with a woman scorned—or pissed.

Triton pushed Rick past the receptionist and into the elevator. Joe followed them inside and hit the lobby button. The doors closed on Rick's face, frozen in a state of shock and embarrassment. Actually Triton was surprised that the guy expressed any embarrassment whatsoever. He was sure it was just momentary.

The ride down to the first floor was taking forever. Awkward silence filled the elevator as the tool looked to Triton and Joe and tried to play off his pathetic excuse for a display.

"Who needs 'em, right, fellas?" Rick asked in some

asinine attempt at male bonding, like they were his buddies from downstairs. "I got ninety-nine problems, but a bitch ain't one. Know what I'm saying?"

"No," Triton said, meaning it in two ways. "I know what Jay-Z's saying, 'cause those are the lyrics from one of his songs." He could tell the guy was seething, but he decided to twist the knife further. It was the first fun he'd had all day. "Now if you had a song, your lyrics might go something like: 'I can't get it up, so my girlfriend did her boss . . . something . . . something to rhyme with boss.' You'll figure it out, but that's a good start."

"It's a great start!" Joe agreed, smiling broadly. "I think the point John's making is: Jay Z's *reality*,"—he made a fist in the air—"Rick's *reality*,"—he let his hand go limp to signify Rick's current problem.

A silly dance tune filled the elevator, but it wasn't Muzak. It was the sad little ring tone from Rick's needlessly tricked-out cell phone. The thing even looked a bit like a penis, which probably helped to make up for Rick's own shortcomings, Triton supposed.

"Hold on," Rick said into the phone before turning his attention directly to Triton. "My *reality*: seven figures and a Ferrari. Your *reality*: minimum wage and a golf cart." He gave a final smug sneer before getting back to the person on the cell phone. "You got The Drake."

The Drake?

"Dude, let me call you back. . . . Because I'm trapped in an elevator with a couple of jackasses, that's why!"

"The Drake" slammed the cell phone shut. Triton considered answering the bastard back about his difference in realities, but Triton didn't really care. A moron like "The Drake" would never understand that some people were proud to work minimum wage if they had the right job. Triton hadn't been raking in the cash as a Marine, but that was all he needed to make him happy. And he didn't even get a golf cart.

True, there were the occasions when he got to ride in the M-1 battle tanks, but it wasn't like the tanks were his.

The elevator doors finally opened and Triton "escorted" Rick out to the lobby. As they passed "The Drake's" two friends, Triton couldn't help but think the guys were idiots for looking like they were surprised by this unexpected turn of events.

"We kindly ask you to leave the premises, sir," Triton said in his most professional tone. It was the same voice he used when speaking to the asshole major who had gotten him drummed out of the service the last time they spoke. Of course, at the time, Triton had still been hoping he had a career in the Marines. He probably wouldn't use that same polite tone with Major Wilson if he were to meet him on the street today.

Rick's buddies hurried to join him at the exit. Triton knew this wasn't going to be good. Guys like "The Drake" were usually at their worst when they had an audience. Particularly an audience like these guys, who were more muscle than brain and hung around "The Drake" because of his money more than his stellar personality.

"Seriously," Rick said as he turned to face Triton, "just spit-balling here. Right outta high school, straight into the Marines. Realized you'd never be all you thought you could be, and that's how you ended up a rent-a-cop. Tell me I'm wrong!"

But Triton had no desire to tell the putz anything. It didn't matter what he thought. All that mattered was getting "The Drake" out of his face. Triton placed his hand on Rick to offer him the door. It was that harmless move that set off "The Drake" and his friends.

All three men took the touch as a personal attack and started up with Triton. The bald guy threw a punch that would have connected with Triton's face had he not pulled back in time. Triton came up with his fists at the ready and rage in his heart. He was not about to let anyone get away with taking a swing at him. But Joe calmly jumped in the middle before it could escalate into a full-fledged brawl.

"Whoa! Whoa! Whoa!" Joe said, directing most of his attention to Triton for some reason. "Okay! All right, then!"

"That genie tried to hit me," Triton said, steaming and staring daggers at the bald guy.

"I saw that, and he shouldn't have done it," Joe said as he turned to the genie. "You shouldn't have done that." Then he turned back to Triton. "But he missed, and you're fine."

Triton was still ready for a fight—wanting one, even. Even crazy extremists were more respectful than these losers. His adrenaline was pumping as it hadn't been for weeks. He hadn't had a chance to take out his aggression on anything but a heavy bag since before he'd been shipped out to Germany.

"John—" Joe's voice got softer and much more calming. "Seriously. We deal with people like this every day, and in order to avoid an incident, sometimes you gotta let it go."

If this was the type of thing Triton was going to go through on a daily basis, he knew that this was not the job for him. That coaching job was looking more and more tempting every moment. He knew that it wouldn't manage to fill the void that leaving the Marines had left him, but at least those children were *actual* children, as opposed to these overgrown infants.

"Yeah," the bald guy said, needlessly chiming in. "Tell your boyfriend to back off."

Joe looked back at the genie. A sarcastic sort of smile came over his face. "Unfortunately for the genie," Joe said, moving away from Triton, "this isn't one of those times."

Somehow without Joe between them, the genie seemed to sense that another attack was the smart thing to do. Once again, he swung at Triton's head, reawakening the ex-Marine's killer persona.

Triton ducked as the genie's fist passed through empty air. He came back up with an elbow that crushed the genie's nose. Blood spurted all over the guy's fancy suit as he fell back and hit the ground. Down and out.

Triton looked to the sharply dressed friend. It

would have ended there as far as Triton was concerned, but Mr. *GQ* was dumb enough to charge at him, throwing weak punches that barely connected. The few times they did, there was nothing behind them.

Growing tired at the pathetic excuse for a fight, Triton lifted the guy off his feet and flung him over a table at "The Drake." The momentum pushed Rick and the guy back through the glass window and out onto the concrete sidewalk.

The crowd in the lobby was stunned. They were all looking at Triton with fear in their eyes. It was the same with the people on the street, who hadn't had any warning before the pair of men came crashing out at them. Joe could only shake his head in disbelief.

As the glass continued to fall onto the concrete, John was suddenly horrified by what he had just done. It was one thing to throw people through windows in the middle of downtown Baghdad. It was quite another to be doing that kind of thing in South Carolina. Immediately, his mind went to Kate. He hadn't imagined anything like this would have happened when she warned him against starting the job so soon after returning home.

Outside, Rick was pulling himself up off the ground. He was covered in glass. "Aw, it's on now!" he screamed, spitting with anger. "See, you really messed up! Somewhere, somehow, somebody just got this on video! By the time you go to sleep tonight, I'm gonna own this building! And tomorrow, don't be late 'cause when you clock in, you're fired!"

Triton just stood by the broken window for a moment as he calmed himself. Yes, it was true that he had scared even himself a little with his rage. But the part that scared him just a bit more was the fact that he didn't feel sorry for what he had done in the least.

10

Triton didn't have much of an appetite, but he took a small bite from the burger anyway. He needed some protein after the day he'd had. Joe, on the other hand, didn't seem to have any problem with the food intake at the moment. He was consuming an unusually large amount of food, even by his usual standards. Triton suspected that Joe was trying to keep his mouth full so they could avoid any awkward conversation. They hadn't really said much to each other since "The Drake" went flying through the glass.

Joe was surprisingly astute at times. For instance, it was his suggestion to stop off at the restaurant for dinner. He had said he'd wanted to go out because he had missed his friend and wanted to spend some more time catching up, as if they hadn't just spent the entire day together sitting around with nothing do to but catch up. That had taken up the first few hours. The great Soloflex/Bowflex debate had taken up the middle of the day, such as it was. And the end of the day was what they were busy not talking about over dinner.

No, Triton knew the real reason for the meal invite. It was so he didn't have to go home and tell Kate what had happened. He didn't have to be greeted at the door with his wife wondering why he came home so early. Asking why there was a spot of blood—not his—on his new shirt.

So they sat back at dinner with their clip-on ties off and shirts unbuttoned, relaxing like the two old friends that they were. But specifically not talking about anything. Triton knew it couldn't last.

After swallowing a particularly impressive bite of food, Joe apparently decided that he was going to have to bring up the elephant in the room. But in typical Joe fashion he made it into a joke by raising his glass in a toast.

"To 'The Drake,' " he said, "and his little problem."

Triton forced a smile and toasted along with his friend. Joe was a good guy. He was always there to lighten the load. That kind of humor was needed more often than not when in the company of John Triton.

"Listen, about today—" Triton started to say, but honestly he didn't know how to continue. He wasn't used to letting people down. He didn't like it either.

"I told you not to worry about it," Joe said. "This is not the first time I got suspended. And somehow I doubt it will be the last."

Triton took another small bite of his food. He knew Joe wasn't kidding. Some people aspire to complacency in life. Joe was one of those people. There was no doubt in Triton's mind that—after nine years—Joe was perfectly happy avoiding a management position, and today's actions certainly helped in that goal.

It didn't make it any easier to know that he had let his friend down, though. Joe had vouched for him. Joe had been excited to be working together; two old friends hanging out every day, like they did back in school.

It also didn't help Triton with the larger issue that Triton had been dealing with ever since that moment Colonel Braun handed him the envelope with his marching papers.

The worst part of the day was the condescending talk he received from the balding and overweight head of security. The former cop had apparently given his all during the years on the force and looked at the security gig as his retirement plan. He didn't like it when people made his day difficult. He had attempted to give Triton some sort of dressing-down.

Triton had almost considered it funny. He had only been defending himself. True, things got out of hand, but in the end it was still some tool getting thrown through a window. The guy didn't even get a scratch, from what Triton could tell, thanks to the tempered glass. None of that seemed to matter. Not that he had said a word in his own defense at the time. He just stood there, taking it, wondering how long before he could get out of that building and unbutton the shirt that had been cutting into his neck all day long.

Eventually he had to tune the guy out entirely. It was impossible to stand there and take it over such a stupid thing. Even when Triton made the conscious choice to disobey orders back in Afghanistan—a much more serious crime, in his opinion—Colonel Braun had never disrespected him the way his former boss had that afternoon.

"No," Triton insisted, "it's not that." He was upset that Joe got suspended because of his actions, but that wasn't the problem pressing on him at the moment.

"Johnny. C'mon, it's no big deal, man," Joe said. "You'll find another job. You have all that training."

John didn't know what his friend was talking about. "Training?" Then he realized, Joe didn't fully appreciate the situation. Triton decided to clear some things up, ticking off his "training" on his fingers. "Let's see . . . covert reconnaissance . . . close-quarter hand-to-hand combat . . . demolitions. Not a big call in the normal workplace for skills like that, Joe."

"John, you're a smart guy," Joe said, his food forgotten. "You could do something else. Whatever you wanted to do."

Triton's face began to harden. The Marine at his core was taking control. "You don't get it, Joe. It's not just *work*. It's not just a *job*. Being a Marine means something to me; it gives me purpose. It's who I am." The reality of the situation came down on him like an avalanche. He had never said what he was about to say out loud before. "Well . . . who I was."

Triton took a sip of his beer. "Now I'm working some bullshit security job . . . Which, by the way, I was just fired from." Triton's eyes narrowed. On top of everything else, he realized that he just insulted his best friend. "Sorry, man."

But Joe just shrugged it off, taking no offense. He was far more interested in his friend's anguish.

"I just don't know what to do," Triton continued. "Everything I worked for my whole life . . . It's all gone. It's over."

"Listen, John," Joe said, sounding more serious than Triton had ever heard him before. "I'm not going to pretend that I know what you're going through, because I don't."

Triton appreciated that. He honestly did. He wasn't sure what he would have said if his friend had tried to pull that "I understand how you feel" crap. The Corps was a calling that not every Marine even truly understood.

"Yeah, your time as a Marine, that's over," Joe acknowledged. "And that sucks, man. But your life is not over, John. It's just changing, and you gotta learn to change with it. Sometimes it's good to take a step back and see what you still have."

Triton nodded as he absorbed Joe's sentiments. Words of wisdom from an unlikely source.

He thought that's what he had been doing all day while sitting on his ass. It had seemed like he was trying to figure things out at the time. But in truth, he had just been wallowing. It was understandable, but it wasn't productive. It wasn't what he was trained to do. John did have important things in his life. Important people. One was sitting across the table from him. But the most important part of his life was waiting at home for him.

"You know, I think I'm going to go home and see my wife," he said.

"Good idea," Joe said.

In the look shared between the two men was a bond and an understanding; the kind that only came from years of friendship. They both stood, leaving their food behind, Triton's barely touched, and reached for their wallets.

"I got this one, man," Joe said, waving off his friend. "You're unemployed, remember?"

They shared a lighthearted laugh as Joe threw more money down on the table than was probably necessary to cover the bill. Triton was glad that they could just up and leave like that. He suddenly needed to get home to Kate.

The two old friends shuffled to the exit together and got into Joe's car. He had offered to drive that morning, since Triton and Kate were still a one-car family. Until he got a job to cover things, it looked like they'd be that way a while longer.

As they rode home in silence, Triton couldn't help but notice Joe took the long way this time. This wasn't about stalling, though. It was clear from the moment that Joe turned onto Foxhill Road why he was going this way.

"You're doing this on purpose, aren't you?" Triton asked.

"What? Driving?" Joe asked, playing innocent. "Yes. I'm driving with purpose. The purpose of going home."

Triton's eyes narrowed. "I mean, that." He pointed out the window to the high school football field. He had not seen it since he last shipped out. The place hadn't changed at all since he and Joe played there not a decade earlier.

"Oh," Joe said, continuing his innocent act, "I didn't even notice where we were. Hey, maybe we should throw the ball around this weekend. Believe it or not, the boss thinks I'm a bit out of shape. Which is funny when you consider—"

"So, you think I should take the coaching job?" Triton asked as they continued on past the field.

"Beats me," Joe said as he turned back toward Triton's home.

"That part of my life is over," Triton said.

"Man, you've got this all-or-nothing personality," Joe said. "You know that? Same as when you were on that field. Turning down a free ride playing college ball to join the Marines. Not that you needed that ride. Daddy could've paid the whole way."

"Books weren't my thing," Triton said. "You know that. I was good at ball. But I was great at being a Marine."

"That's why I strive for mediocrity," Joe said. "I'm happy just getting up in the morning and having a place to go."

"I guess that's the difference between you and me," Triton said, realizing that it came out a bit more condescending than he had intended it.

"Well, you know what they say about opposites attracting," Joe said as he pulled up in from of Triton's house. "Who knows? Maybe now that you're back, we'll rub off on each other a bit more."

"Don't know if I want you rubbing anything on me," Triton said, giving his friend a light punch in the shoulder.

Joe reacted as if Triton had just broken his arm.

The pair said their good-byes as Triton popped out of the car, slamming the door behind him. But Joe wasn't done with him just yet.

"You okay?" he asked, one last time.

Triton took a moment to actually think about the question.

"No," he said, honestly, but there was a feeling of hope inside him. One that he hadn't felt until that moment, realizing he had a good friend and a great wife supporting him. "But I will be."

"That's my boy," Joe said.

Triton waved as Joe drove off. He then turned to face his house. The lights were on. Kate was home from school and her last final. He knew she was probably hitting the books to get a jump on the summer session classes that started up in a few weeks.

She was the one person he knew with the same amount of drive that he possessed. Oddly enough, they had both found ways to use saving lives as an outlet for their passions. He wasn't looking forward to going inside and telling Kate that she had been right when she suggested he take some time to get his head straight.

Now that his father was no longer in his life, she was the one person he hated letting down the most.

11

Morgan could not believe his damned luck.

Everyone else was out celebrating. The heist had gone perfectly. Okay, well, there was that tiny glitch afterward with the cop car, but they got away clean, so what did it matter? Now was the time to party and enjoy the spoils of their victory. And where was Morgan? In a cab riding through the seediest downtown area he had ever seen. And he had seen some seedy downtown areas in his time.

Warehouses and auto body shops lined the urban street. It was desolate, not the kind of place he wanted to be at night. But this was his punishment, Rome had said. This is what he got for taking out the police car. As far as Morgan was concerned, he should have been rewarded for a job well done. He should be feasting on steak with everyone else.

Then again, if he wanted to continue to enjoy his newfound wealth, *someone* had to do what he was doing. He couldn't exactly enjoy a proper meal behind bars.

The taxi pulled up to one of the oldest and most dilapidated-looking buildings. Morgan handed his money to the driver and got out of the cab. The cabbie peeled out without waiting for Morgan to get safely inside. He couldn't blame the driver. Morgan wouldn't want to be witness to anything that happened in this neighborhood either.

He glanced up and down the street. It was empty, but that was even more unnerving. He approached the closed-down garage. There was no activity going on around it. For a moment he thought maybe he wasn't expected. The last time Morgan had been here, it was daytime and there were people on the street around him. Not like this area was a popular hangout, but at least the homeless had been up and around.

Morgan moved to the steel door beside the closed metal roll-down garage. The windows in the door and in the building were blacked out and covered with steel bars. *Not very welcoming*. He glanced up at the small camera mounted above the door and pressed the intercom button.

"*Yeah*," a muffled voice came back over the intercom. Morgan recognized the voice as belonging to the proprietor of the fine establishment, though it sounded like the guy was eating something and hadn't bothered to swallow before speaking.

"It's Morgan," he replied, looking up at the security camera.

"*So?*" Frank shot back.

"So what?" Morgan asked. It was pretty obvious that he wanted Frank to buzz him the hell in.

"*What's the password?*" Frank asked.

"Password?" Morgan couldn't believe this guy. He didn't know about any password. Didn't care, either. "The password is 'kiss my ass'—now open the damned door. I hate this neighborhood. It's got rats, stray dogs, and who knows what else."

Apparently that was good enough for Frank, because Morgan heard the familiar click of the lock being undone as he was buzzed into the building.

The atmosphere inside the shop was distinctly different from outside. On the street, the building had looked abandoned and forgotten. Within its walls was a different story entirely.

The shop was buzzing with activity. Heavily tattooed mechanics, pros at the chop-shop game, were busy working like surgeons cutting up Porsches, BMWs, and Ferraris. Sparks flew from steel saws taking apart fenders and wheel mounts. The workers peeled away layers of the vehicles, exposing more and more of their metal innards.

Morgan stepped inside the building, shutting the door behind him. Even in the cacophony of metal upon metal he could hear the distinct click of the lock behind him. After only a couple steps, he found himself face to face with Devon, a huge thug even by Morgan's standards. The guy was sporting an IMI Desert Eagle in a shoulder holster. Morgan was suitably impressed. As Rome had recently learned, Morgan had an interest in weaponry.

"Arms up," Devon said by way of a greeting.

Morgan did as instructed, though he didn't like it

much. "Why you gotta frisk me every time I come here? This is 'cause I'm black, right?"

"Yeah," Devon said casually as he patted Morgan down.

Morgan put up with the demeaning display, but he didn't enjoy it. He especially didn't like the fact that Devon's hands seemed to be lingering far longer than necessary in certain areas.

Once the indignity was finished, Morgan brushed his clothes smooth. "Wash your hands first next time," he said. "I just got this out of the cleaners."

Morgan turned away from Devon to see Frank exiting his small office. The man was chewing on a hoagie as he walked toward Morgan. He wiped his right hand on his pants and held it out. "Morgan, my brutha from another mutha. What's happenin'?"

Morgan looked at Frank and his greasy hand with disgust. There was no way in hell he was touching the man. Frank seemed to get the message, since he dropped his hand to his side.

"Did Rome love the Mercedes?" Frank asked. "Wasn't that a sweet ride? Where is it, out front?"

"We had to dump it," Morgan explained simply.

Frank's eyes nearly popped right out of his head. After the password and the pat-down, Morgan couldn't have cared less.

"Dump it?" Frank asked, losing his cool and yelling over the noise of the chop shop. "Are you insane? That car was worth two hundred easy."

"It was a right-hand drive, Frank," Morgan said

coolly. "Used in the commission of a major felony. That blends right in, doesn't it?"

Morgan briefly considered telling Frank the location of the parking garage where they had dumped the car. He could always go and pick it up on his own later if he was so inclined. But then if he got caught, it would lead directly back to Rome and the crew, so Morgan kept quiet.

Frank wiped the sweat from his upper lip. "Okay, I hear ya. I thought it was unique. I know Rome likes a little flash when he's working."

"*Flash*," Morgan said, "not a neon sign."

"Okay, okay," Frank relented. He moved behind the cars being chopped. Morgan took that to mean he should follow.

"I got the perfect getaway car right over here," he said as he moved to the corner of the shop. The building layout was in an L shape, causing Morgan to wonder just how far it went back. "Just came in this afternoon."

Morgan grinned as they made their way past the BMWs and Porsches. Each of the cars was flashier than the next, but not quite the attention-grabbers of their original ride. Maybe he'd come back here and make a purchase of his own once he got his share of the profits. Frank would probably cut him a good deal, what with their newfound business relationship and the low overhead of the man's operation.

Morgan pulled himself out of his musings as they stepped around the corner and he laid his eyes on the vehicle Frank had in mind.

"A minivan?" Morgan asked incredulously as his eyes fell on the Ford Aerostar. "Do I look like a soccer mom to you? What about that one over there?" He pointed back toward a Porsche.

Frank snorted. "Where are you all gonna fit, in the glove compartment?" He walked around the minivan as if he was a used-car salesman, pointing out all the extras that came with purchase. "No one's gonna give you a second look in this. It's got stow-and-go seating, built-in DVD player, and it's economical."

"It's a damned minivan," Morgan repeated. He didn't care if it got a hundred miles to the gallon. They only needed something to get them out of town. "Black men don't drive minivans. It's *unblack*."

"I could throw in some spinners if you want," Frank added.

Morgan shot Frank a withering look. He wasn't sure if Frank was messing with him or not, nor did he care. Frank seemed to get the message because he backed away and took another bite from his dripping hoagie.

"The keys are in it," Frank said through a mouthful of bread, meat, and oil. "Just drive it out. The garage door's automatic." He turned away from Morgan and headed back to his office. Probably to finish off a beer with his dinner. "Enjoy!" he yelled back as he walked away.

Morgan was dripping with frustration. He walked up to the minivan's door and glanced inside. It was just too much. A pair of damned plastic baby shoes were hanging from the rearview mirror. Morgan cringed. But as he looked through the big glass windows, something caught his eye just past the suburban nightmare.

A forest green Cadillac was parked near the garage door. It was big and beautiful, and Morgan could practically hear it calling to him.

Ignoring the minivan, Morgan moved over to the Caddy. The keys were dangling from the ignition. The car was just waiting to be taken out on the road.

Morgan smiled. "Now this is what a brutha's talkin' about."

He popped the driver's door open and slid inside. The plush leather seat formed around his ass as if it was designed for him exclusively. He slid his hands over the wheel. There wasn't a blemish in the smooth leather.

The car was perfect. Showy, but not too eye-catching. It screamed politely of class. This car would certainly catch some eyes, but no one would be suspicious of it.

Morgan turned the key and started the engine. It didn't quite purr like the Mercedes had, but it wasn't half bad. He put the car in drive and rolled it to the garage door, setting off the motion sensor. The door rose, ushering the car out into the world.

Morgan pulled out onto the street. Once he turned the corner, he burned rubber, accelerating into the distance with a grin on his face that almost lit the interior.

12

Rome pushed the hotel room door open without separating his lips from Angela's. It had already been a wild night of celebrating, and now he had some partying of a more personal nature in store. Once they were inside the room and the door was shut behind them, they finally broke the kiss that had started at the elevator.

There were some in the group—well, only Vescera really—who had thought that dining out in public to enjoy the success of the heist had been a bad idea. But hiding in plain sight was exactly the point. Rome knew that the police were busy with roadblocks, expecting them to head straight out of the city after such a brazen robbery. All the more reason for them to go out on the town instead. No one would be looking for them at one of the finest restaurants in town.

The plan was to give things a day to cool down. Then they could easily roll out of town when the cops already thought he was gone. Besides, Rome had an appointment to keep tomorrow just outside of town.

They'd be leaving around checkout time, like any other travelers. Rome would have preferred to get a bit more distance—time-wise—from the robbery, but it was just as dangerous to stick around the city, especially with a guy like Morgan on the team. Rome liked Morgan, both in spite of and because of his unpredictable nature, but he wasn't going to take too many risks with the guy.

Angela left Rome's side and went to the bar to make some drinks. It made sense for her to be so comfortable in the room, since she was sharing it with him. Bennett, Vescera, and Morgan were scattered in rooms throughout the hotel so that if the cops came, there was a better chance that some of them could escape. They didn't want to make it too easy to get a hold of the entire group by staying on the same floor. Then again, the guys didn't want to be too far from the diamonds either.

Angela slipped behind Rome and slid his jacket off his shoulders. Her moves were sensual and deliberate. Rome could sense there was something more than passion in her gentle touch. She was warming him up to hit him with the question he knew she was waiting to ask.

"What happened today?" she asked, softly, into his ear.

"We made a lot of money," he replied simply. Rome knew what she was asking, and he had hoped to dismiss the subject quickly. Angela was smart enough not to bring it up in front of the others, but now that they were alone, he knew she'd want some answers. He veered away from the plan without discussing it with her first. In his list of crimes, it wasn't exactly the worst, but it was bad enough, from her perspective at least.

Rome sat down in the large comfortable chair the hotel provided, wishing that she would switch topics.

"In the vault," Angela gently pressed on. It was clear that she was attempting to broach the topic carefully. "With the kid?"

Angela moved around the chair, kissing him. She was trying to loosen him up, to keep him calm. She worked her way around the chair and draped her leg over him, straddled him, waiting for an answer.

"The kid showed he couldn't keep his mouth shut," Rome replied. That part he hadn't had any second thoughts over. A guy like that couldn't be trusted once the cops came around. He knew Rome's name and had already shown that it could slip out when least expected. Besides, Rome already knew how he was going to spend the small share that he had saved in getting rid of the kid.

"And Morgan?" she continued anxiously. "Killing the cop?"

Rome took a moment with that question. He still wasn't sure what to do about Morgan. In one shot, the guy managed to take things to a whole other level. And yet, part of Rome still got a kick out of the fireworks. It was quite the capper on what he considered the perfect crime.

"He just went a little overboard," Rome replied, knowing what an understatement that was. But he did have to take some responsibility as well. "And in all fairness to Morgan, I *was* firing an automatic weapon at that cop."

Angela rubbed against his body, but continued to gently prod him with the questions. "Murders? Dead cops? Doesn't that pose a potential problem for us?" She didn't want him to realize how nervous she actually was, but questioning him repeatedly only showed her unease.

Man, she was being a buzz kill. As much as he was enjoying her attention, she was starting to piss him off with her talk. Rome didn't like being questioned and decided to put an end to that part of the evening. "So does a prison term. The bottom line is, we got away clean."

He looked into Angela's eyes, not quite sure he liked what he was seeing there. "What's the problem, Angela? Don't you trust me anymore?"

She turned away from him, silently. Though he had asked his questions with a playful tone, he was expecting an answer, and he didn't like to have to wait for it. Angela's silence was getting to him. He needed to know that he could trust her.

"Look at me, Angela," he said roughly. Playtime was over . . . or at least on a break.

Angela looked him right in the eye. He was impressed by the strength of her stare. She wasn't afraid of him. But at the same time, he could see that she was captivated by him. She was enveloped by his strength in the same way that he was in hers.

"The kid knew my name. That's dangerous . . . for

all of us," he continued, still to no response. "Baby, is there anything in these eyes that makes you think I could ever hurt you?"

Angela surprised him by continuing to look deeply into his eyes as if she was actually going to find an answer in there. But the moment was only brief. He could tell by the way her body relaxed in his grasp and her lips parted that her doubts were quickly erased. She softly shook her head no.

"I'd die for you," she said.

"And I'd kill for you," he said. And meant it.

They kissed again. This time, the passion held no questions. There were no ulterior motives. They melted together, finally on the same page. It was ferocious. Rome didn't want it to end. His thoughts were so full of Angela at the moment, he barely heard the ring of his cell phone.

Rome briefly considered letting the call roll to voice mail, but knew it could be important. He didn't want to be making love to Angela while one of the crew was calling to alert him that the cops were about to bust down his door.

"What?" he asked.

"Forget what you did in the store," a male voice replied, skipping the pleasantries. The voice was disguised, but Rome knew who it was. His "silent partner" went to ridiculous lengths to protect himself, but Rome understood paranoia.

"You killed a cop," the voice continued, "and that's a problem."

115

"I'll send flowers," Rome replied, tired of talking about this particular subject. He put up with Angela because he actually had feelings for her. He wasn't about to explain himself to anyone else. "Relax. We meet tomorrow. You get your diamonds, I get my money."

Rome closed his cell phone, disconnecting the call without another word. He had more important things to do at the moment than deal with a silent partner who didn't want to remain silent.

"We'll see him tomorrow," Rome felt the need to explain. "He'll be fine."

"Jackass," she said. Angela didn't like having more people than necessary on a job. The problem was that without their silent partner, there wouldn't have even been a job. That kind of made him a bit more than just *necessary* in this particular case.

"Never get emotional in business," Rome said, with a deep kiss. "It clouds your judgment."

"Only two things that get me going emotionally," Angela said between kisses, "money and sex."

Rome knew that the money would come tomorrow. So for tonight, that only left . . .

The phone rang again.

This time he figured it could roll over to the automatic voice message system. But it would keep ringing all night if he didn't answer. If he just turned it off, there'd be a dozen voice mails waiting. The last thing he needed was a series of calls from the same number adding to the small amount of evidence he had left behind in their heist.

Rome finally took the call, but didn't quite answer it right away. He ignored the party on the other end as he continued kissing Angela. He figured the guy on the line would wait if he really wanted to talk.

Eventually—and regretfully—Rome slid Angela off him. He moved out to the balcony, where he could have some privacy. It wasn't like he needed to keep the call a secret from Angela. He'd probably tell her everything as soon as he hung up. Or maybe later. But it was just easier to conduct business when he wasn't doing it in front of an audience. Rome moved the phone to his ear as he looked over the panoramic view of the city lights.

"Don't start with me," he finally said into the phone.

"You've lost control," the familiarly distorted voice said.

"See, that's where you're wrong," Rome replied. "I've *gained* control."

"Is that right?"

"You bet your ass that's right. I have the diamonds, therefore I have the power."

There was silence on the other end of the line for a moment as his partner took in what he was saying.

"You have no idea the level of hell I can bring down on you," his silent partner finally said.

Rome knew it was an empty threat. He could cause far more problems for his partner than the other way around. Not to say that his partner couldn't make life more difficult in ways that Rome had no intention of experiencing.

"Yeah, but you won't," Rome replied. "Not if you want to see these diamonds."

Frustration all but oozed through the phone. Rome relished the fact that he was calling the shots. It was a position that suited him well. He still needed the guy on the other end of the line to move the merchandise. Sure, Rome could've done that part himself, but it was easier this way. Rome had already done the heavy lifting. It was someone else's turn to finish the job.

"*Tomorrow, noon,*" said the distorted voice. "*I get my diamonds. You get your money.*" And then he was gone. There was nothing but dial tone, as if cutting off the conversation had given him the upper hand.

Rome just laughed silently. Everything was going exactly as planned.

13

Kate couldn't stop wondering about John's first day long enough to actually absorb the words on the page in front of her. Thankfully her last final had been that morning. Now she was just reading ahead to get a jump on next semester. If she had really been studying, she wouldn't have had the TV on in the background.

John had sounded fine when they'd spoken that morning, right after her final. Well, actually he had sounded bored. He didn't have that rush in his voice that he had when she spoke to him at work as a Marine. Even when he was just stationed on base, she could always tell that he was excited just to be in the uniform. He had none of that this morning. But maybe it would come with time. She tried to convince herself of that as she went back to her reading.

She still couldn't manage to pay attention to the book.

When Kate heard the front door open, she forgot the words entirely. Inside, she felt the same surge of excitement that she had when she heard the same sound the day before. John was home. And he was home for good. She had never really known the feel of that last part for their entire marriage.

She wondered when the excitement of John simply coming through a door was going to go away. At what point would it be normal that John was simply coming home at the end of the day again? She hoped that she never completely lost the feel of it.

"Hi, baby. How was work?" she asked as she greeted him. Before she could even give him a kiss, she knew something was wrong. John wasn't an emotional man, which made it all the more difficult for him to hide when he was upset. "What? What happened?"

"Nothing." Triton shrugged off her concern, which worried her even more. He didn't normally shut down on her like that. There was more to the story.

Kate didn't want to press, but she wasn't about to let it slide. So she waited for John to come around on his own. It only took a moment.

"Just . . . stuff," Triton added, as if that explained anything.

In the silence that followed, Kate couldn't help but notice that the news was running an amateur video showing a man flying through a glass window at a downtown building. The voiceover answered her question: "They're hired to protect us, but who protects us from them? Security guards out of control. Tonight at eleven."

Kate didn't have to see the blurry image of her husband on the screen to know that his day had gone far worse than she ever imagined it could.

"*Stuff*?" she asked, trying not to sound like she was judging him. "Like you throwing a guy through a window?"

"Yeah," Triton said, "that and some other stuff."

Kate could only assume that the "other stuff" was that he didn't have the job Joe had gotten him anymore. She didn't much mind that part. It was never right for him in the first place. But she wasn't the type for "I told you so." She was much more concerned about how John was taking it. Before last week, he had never been fired from anything before. She worried how much his discharge from the Marines was going to affect his everyday life now.

She tried to lighten the mood, though. "I thought my days of worrying about you were over. What happened?"

Kate followed John as he collapsed on the couch. He made a show of taking off his tie and unbuttoning his shirt. She figured he had probably put it back on during the car ride home for her sake. She knew John well enough to know the shirt came undone the moment he left the building. Especially when the shirt was this tight. When Joe had sent it over, she had known in an instant the thing was too small, but apparently that was all they had in stock at the moment.

"This isn't me," he said.

Again, this wasn't the place to remind him that she had told him the same thing a day earlier. But she did need him to understand that it wasn't the end of the world. "You jumped into it the minute you got back. You need some time."

"What was I supposed to do, Kate? Just come home and sit around?" he asked, and she knew he was honestly searching for an answer. "That's not me either. I can't do that."

"I know you can't, but you didn't give yourself any time."

"Time? For what?"

"For you . . . for me . . . for us," she said. "To figure things out."

Kate had taken the week off from work so that they could spend time together. All she had to do was get past her last final that morning, and she would have nothing but John to keep her occupied. She hadn't even had the chance to tell him about her time off when he had called about the job Joe had secured for him. It had caught her by surprise. Had she known what he was up to, she would have called Joe to see if there was any way to give John a couple days before starting. She knew it was more John's idea to throw himself into a new job. Kate had been more than a little upset to learn that he had taken the job so quickly and planned to start the day after he returned.

But now, she wasn't going to give him the chance to make other plans. She had the time, and she had the solution to at least one part of his problem.

"What if we took off?" she said as soon as the idea came to her. Going someplace was the plan all along, but she had never had the chance to discuss it with John. She hadn't even had the time to plan it.

"What?"

"Just leave," she said, her mind working on the idea. "Go. Something crazy."

She could tell he was considering it. But she knew that she just couldn't let him think too much about it, or he'd talk himself out of it before he ever made a decision.

"We'll get up in the morning, and we'll just go," she said, barreling forward with the idea. Neither of them had ever been this spontaneous before. Between her job at the hospital and his time in the Marines, they never had the luxury of just waking up and deciding to go on an adventure. But now there was nothing stopping them.

"Where?"

"I don't know where," she said, debating on the beach or the mountains or a half-dozen other places they could get to by car on the spur of the moment. It didn't matter where they went as long as they were together. "Anywhere. It doesn't matter . . . Come on . . . I've given this a lot of thought."

"Oh, you have?" John asked, not believing her. She didn't blame him, since the idea was fairly spur-of-the-moment.

"Yeah," she said playfully as she bounced up onto her knees on the couch. "What do you think? Just you and me. I want to do this. Say yes . . . please say yes!"

John seemed to consider the idea, but she could tell he was just milking it. He had made his decision and was just stringing her along.

"Okay, yes," he said.

Kate threw herself at her husband. She was ecstatic. The two of them hadn't spent any real time alone together since before the last time he'd shipped out. And even then, it was only a long weekend in the house together. With the exception of their abbreviated honeymoon, this was the first time that they really were going away together.

"Yes," she said, feeling immensely triumphant. She hadn't realized until just this moment how much *she* needed to get away too.

The celebratory kissing grew more passionate, moving from playful to sensual in seconds. She ripped off his security shirt—knowing that he'd never need it again—and caressed his body underneath. This time, they didn't make it out of the living room.

14

The squad room was buzzing with activity. Officers were on the phone and on the radios, coordinating with those in the field. Highway patrol was involved, and a few people had even suggested contacting the FBI. The police force took things very seriously when one of their own was murdered. The entire investigation was being coordinated through Detective Van Buren, and he wouldn't have it any other way.

The detective checked the map posted on the bulletin board. It showed the entire county, with pins noting where the police were focusing the search. The only thing they really had to go on was that the car looked fancy and expensive. "Like one of those imports," the guy at the coffee stand had said. It wasn't much to go on.

Van Buren took one of the pins off the highway and moved it to another part of the map. He had directed that team to search an area of town known for its shadier pawnshops. The detective had a pretty good idea that none of the tiny operations would have the ability to move twelve million dollars worth of diamonds. Actually, he knew full well the exact kind of fence that type of job would require. Having worked in law enforcement as long as he had, Van Buren had much more familiarity with the criminal element than when he had started. But he needed to keep the investigation moving.

His superiors were already giving him a hard time about the lack of leads since the theft and the subsequent murder of Officer Stein. He could have worked a bit harder with all of the witnesses to make sure their stories matched up, but time was of the essence in a case like this. Every move Van Buren made had to be well calculated to be sure the investigation was moving in the direction he wanted it to go.

The city leaders were also putting in their two cents, which sufficiently complicated matters. When a cop was killed, it wasn't just the other boys in blue that cared. The mayor's office had been calling every hour on the hour for an update. The flow of information was tying up a number of officers and keeping them off the investigation, but Van Buren wasn't about to say anything. It would help to have the mayor's office upset. Besides, as much as the mayor's people assured him that their concern was for finding the cop killers, he couldn't help but think they also had tourism and the city's overall crime rate more in mind.

"The tip line just sent in another dozen possibles," Charlie said as he hung up the phone and handed the list to Van Buren.

"Check 'em out," Van Buren said, giving the list back without even looking at it.

"All of them?" Charlie asked. "I mean, some of these—"

"When was the last time an officer died in the line around here?" Van Buren asked abruptly. He knew that his anger was misplaced, but he couldn't help that at the moment. "I want to make sure that we're doing everything we can to locate these killers."

It was supposed to be a simple jewel heist. He certainly didn't have all this in mind when he'd offered to take the call from Charlie less than twenty-four hours earlier. Van Buren didn't have a real problem with the work. He liked the mental exercise. There was a tremendous amount of coordination to see that the police were covering the areas he needed them to cover. He *was* running a textbook search.

The entire precinct was now working on the case, as opposed to the handful that would have been involved in a simple high-end robbery. Guys had even come in on their days off to help find Officer Stein's killer. And every one of them was currently reporting to Van Buren. Not a move was made in the state that he didn't have control over. It was a nice feeling of power, he had to admit to himself as he glanced back at the map.

"The department's going to be spread a little thin," Charlie said. "Even with all the extra help we've got on this."

"We've already pulled back the roadblocks," Van Buren said. "If they managed to get past our net already, then they're long gone. It's time to start scouring the city."

"They wouldn't be dumb enough to stick around, would they?" Charlie asked.

"Oh, I got a feeling these guys are plenty dumb," Van Buren said. "The only reason we haven't caught them yet is because they're laying low. It's time to smoke them out."

"This is a nice hotel," Rome said after he had dropped his keycard off in the express checkout box. All of their rooms had been reserved under false names, using fake credit cards, so it wasn't like he needed to stick around for a receipt. "Shame we can't stay a few more days without risking a longer sojourn in a less hospitable place."

"We can always come back," Angela said. "Sometime in the future."

"No," Rome said as he took the velvet pouch out of his pocket and rolled it around in his hands. "I think I'm done with South Carolina for a while. Time to go out and explore the world. Maybe a nice vacation in the islands. I can get used to this lifestyle. Work one day a year. Make enough to support me for the other three-sixty-four."

"Do you really think it's a good idea to have that out?" Angela asked. Her eyes drifted down to the bag of diamonds in his hands.

"Relax," Rome said. "It's just a fancy pouch. Nothing to call attention to us."

"Certainly nothing like a grenade launcher," Angela said.

"Don't start that again, dear," Rome said as he indicated down the hall, where Bennett, Vescera, and Morgan were all stepping out of the elevator. "At least, not in front of the kids."

Rome watched as Bennett and Vescera dropped their keycards into the express checkout box. Morgan took a minute to locate his keycard—checking all his pockets and unintentionally revealing his gun to anyone looking—before he dropped it into the box and joined the others.

"Man, I could go for some breakfast," Morgan said as he reached the group.

"That was what room service was for," Rome reminded him. "So someone else would pay for it. Remember? Part of the reason we used those credit cards for check-in was to stay anonymous *and* put our expenses on them."

Morgan looked back to the express checkout box. "You mean I have to break back into the room just so I can order some food? Can I at least get some coffee?"

"We'll stop on the way out of town," Rome said as he started for the door to the parking garage.

"What are we ridin' today? Lexus? BMW?" Vescera asked as they made their way through the rows of parked cars. "I could get used to this. Maybe test out something new so I know what to buy with my sudden windfall."

"Um . . . not exactly," Morgan said as they stopped

at the car he had picked up the night before. "I got us something a little less flashy. But still with some style."

"A Caddy?" Vescera said as he took in the car.

"You don't know what we coulda been riding," Morgan said. Rome could tell the guy was hurt that they didn't like his choice of vehicle.

"You'd prefer a lime green Pinto?" Rome asked, throwing a comforting arm around Morgan. "We're going for unobtrusive, right, man?"

Morgan's face lit up as he nodded.

"So let me get this straight," Bennett said, laughing softly. "Yesterday, when we all had considerably smaller bank accounts, we were in the pimped-out rich ride. Today, when are coffers are seriously busting out, we're in the plain-Jane Caddy. There's something wrong with this picture."

"Last I checked, we haven't made one thin dime yet," Rome said as he slipped the diamonds back in his pocket. "And we won't if we go around in a car that will grab everyone's attention."

"I'm not complaining," Bennett said. "I'm just saying—"

"Shotgun!" Morgan piped up.

"Um, I think the *lady* will be riding up front with me," Rome said.

"No," Morgan said. "Um . . . I meant, I forgot my shotgun. I think I left it in the back of the Mercedes."

Rome wasn't sure whether or not to take Morgan seriously. He just shrugged his shoulders at the rest of the crew, and they all got in the car and pulled out of the hotel's parking garage.

The Cadillac handled well as it hit the streets, but Rome was looking forward to trading up when they reached the exchange point. He was also looking forward to getting rid of some of the excess baggage.

15

Triton grabbed the small cooler Kate had filled with snacks for the road and took it out to the SUV. He was used to long trips with nothing to eat, but he figured she might want something along the way.

They were getting a bit of a later start than they had originally planned. Technically, that was Triton's fault. Kate had wanted to throw a quick load in the wash before they left. She had looked so cute wearing one of his big T-shirts and nothing else that he couldn't control himself as she loaded the washing machine. It was a good thing they were going away together, because they were running out of rooms in the house to make love in.

Afterward, they had a late breakfast before they decided it was time to head out on the road. The late morning was chilly, but it was nothing compared to the brisk mountain air they would be experiencing the same time the following morning. Kate had wanted to just set out on the road and choose the direction then, but Triton wasn't big on wandering aimlessly, no matter how much Kate's sudden sense of adventure called for them to do that. It may have been a matter of old habits dying hard, but Triton liked to know where he was going when he started any journey.

"You almost ready?" he called out to Kate when he got back in the house.

"Why don't you come and hurry me along?" she called back from the bedroom, where she was finishing getting dressed.

"Somehow I think if I do that, we won't be getting on the road until after dark."

"Good point!" she said with a laugh.

Triton grabbed their duffel bags that were sitting by the front door. He had relented in his strict adherence to planning by allowing Kate not to make any reservations anywhere. She kept saying that reservations ruined the adventure. Personally, Triton felt that reservations just meant they could choose their own adventure instead of having one chosen for them. But he didn't fight it. So they were about to head out with no clue whether they'd find a nice comfortable lodge with a room or they'd be setting up tent on a patch of ground under the beautiful sky.

As much as he liked camping, he was secretly wishing for the comfy lodge. He'd lain on enough ground over the past few years.

Triton threw their two small duffels in the back of the Navigator. The camping equipment was already inside if they needed it. They wouldn't require much else for the week they had planned.

He stood by the SUV waiting for Kate to finish up. As always, she was well worth the wait, coming out in all her morning glory. Her beautiful blond hair practically glowed in the early morning sunlight. She was a vision in denim.

Triton opened the passenger door for her and dared a glance at her butt as she slid inside. When he remembered it was a move like that that had already delayed them once that morning, he quickly focused his attention elsewhere. Making love in the driveway wouldn't go over well with the neighbors.

"You good?" he asked.

"Yeah," she said with a smile brighter than the sun.

Triton closed her door and ran around to his side of the SUV. At first, he'd had to get used to the feel of the vehicle. He hadn't driven anything other than a Jeep or a Humvee in the longest time. Before he could do anything, he readjusted the seat to fit his considerable larger frame and moved the mirrors. Then he started the engine and pulled out of the driveway, making a left-hand turn and heading toward the mountains and a different kind of adventure than the ones he was used to.

Triton wound the vehicle through the residential streets. The roads and sidewalks were pretty empty; most people were at work at that hour. Triton didn't envy his neighbors stuck in their glass buildings on a beautiful day like this. He knew he'd have to worry about finding a job soon enough, but not for another week. When he did start thinking about it again, he knew the top of his list was someplace where he could work outdoors. But he stopped himself before went down that path again. Today was about relaxing . . . and Kate.

Once they were past the Craftsman homes and on the open road, Kate finally pulled out the map from the glove compartment.

"What's this?" Triton asked jokingly. "You suddenly lose that sense of adventure? Need to know where we're going?"

"Well, it wouldn't hurt to have an idea of the destination," Kate said. "I mean, do you really want to end up in some rickety old motel with holes in the walls and mold growing in the bathroom?"

"As long as I'm with you, that place would be paradise," Triton said.

Kate looked over at her husband and burst out laughing.

Triton couldn't hold it any longer and joined her.

"Okay," Triton said once they got over the laughing fit. "Find us someplace nice."

"You got it," she said as she scanned over the map.

Triton was already enjoying himself. Maybe this was all that he needed to get his head on straight. Some time with the most important person in his life was more than enough to keep his mind off his troubles.

"Oh, Mount Cedar," Kate said, recognizing a spot on the map. "We used to go there when I was a kid. My grandparents had a cabin. Grandpa and I used to fish off the dock."

Triton liked the picture he had in his mind. He had

never met Kate's grandfather, but he had seen pictures of them together from when she was a young girl. It sounded nice and homey. And "homey" was very different from his own childhood.

Kate continued with her story. "Later I found out that my dad hid under the dock and put the fish on my hook. It turns out the lake didn't even have fish."

"How old were you?"

"I couldn't have been more than six or seven," she said. "Wow, I haven't thought about that for years."

"Sounds nice."

But Kate had already moved on from the memory and was examining the map more closely. "The mountains are hours away. You sure you don't want to just hang out at the beach?"

"Nah, I think I've seen enough sand," Triton answered. For a moment, he worried that the mention of sand was going to throw him back into his dark spiral, but it didn't. In fact, he was actually enjoying himself. Probably for the first time since he got home. His entire body felt relaxed, and he couldn't be sure, but he thought his lips may have even curled into a bit of a smile.

"Besides," he said playfully, "you're not the only one that has childhood memories of the mountains."

Kate looked at him with a hint of suspicion in her eyes. He didn't blame her, knowing full well that he had never mentioned family trips to the mountains before.

"You guys used to go to Mount Cedar?" she asked, carefully.

136

"Not Mount Cedar," he said, spinning his tale. "It was a little farther up."

He decided to wait it out. Let her doubt the story, as he knew she was doing.

"So, you gonna tell me where?" she finally asked.

"Just this place my dad use to take me and my brothers when we were little," he said, hoping she would go along.

"Was it far?" she asked.

"Pretty far."

"And what did you guys do up there?" she wondered. He could tell she was interested in hearing the details. He had her.

"Nothing really," he said.

"Nothing?" she said, suspiciously. "Was it fun?"

Triton got suddenly still, playing into his tale. "My dad seemed to like it."

Kate let that hang for a moment before prompting him to go on. "Why?"

"Well," Triton said. "It was far enough away that no one could hear us scream."

For the briefest moment, Triton thought that he had truly gotten her. But then she shot him an exasperated look.

"John, you don't have any brothers," she said. He could tell she was irritated with herself for being suckered in.

"No," he admitted. "No. I don't have any brothers . . . That is weird."

"You're weird," she said, giving him a playful swat on the arm.

They shared a pair of devious smiles. It was one of those silly moments only two people in love could truly appreciate.

Of course, the story only made him think of his dad. There hadn't been any vacations to the mountains when he was a kid. There hadn't been many vacations at all. His father was too busy for petty things like spending time with his family. He was far too important for that.

Triton may have been too busy for vacations in the past, but it was never because he thought he was too important to spend time with Kate. Even when the Marines were calling, he had made sure that there was always time for her. That was only one of the differences between him and his father.

Farther down the highway, Triton saw a sign for Manze's Gas Station. He looked down at the gas gauge and saw it was just below a quarter tank. "We've got a long trip ahead of us. Better fill up." He turned into the station, slipping off the highway and into the dust and gravel lot.

Triton pulled the Navigator up to the gas pump. There was a green Cadillac beside them with one guy sitting in the back. Triton hardly paid him any attention as he hopped out of the Navigator, heading for the station's grocery mart.

"Want anything?" he asked Kate, who was staying behind in the SUV.

"Diet Coke," she replied with a small smile as he turned and headed for the store.

He could feel her eyes on him as he walked away from her. He thought he heard her say, "Nice butt," although he wasn't quite sure if she would be so brazen in the middle of a gas station.

He turned and looked back at her. "What?"

"I said, 'I love you,'" she replied with a mischievous grin.

He smiled back. That was definitely not what she had said.

Triton continued on to the gas station store, giving a nod to a man dressed in a suit with his collar undone as he passed.

Rome nodded a polite hello to a rather muscularly oversize local as he went back to the Cadillac. He had to agree that it wasn't as nice as the Mercedes they had yesterday, but it was necessary to switch vehicles. He would have preferred to lose some of the team as well so they weren't as noticeable traveling together, but for some reason the others didn't trust him to collect on their behalf.

It wouldn't be long until he was free of them. In more ways than one. They were on their way to make the exchange that would get them all paid. As best he could tell, the cops didn't have any good pictures of the team. They probably had some vague descriptions, but nothing they could run on the news. The guy in the convenience store didn't recognize them when he, Angela, and Bennett walked in. Vescera was still at the car, and Morgan was currently indisposed. Once they got on the road again, he figured they'd be safe until they reached the drop point. No one had a description of this car.

Rome continued past the SUV and toward the Cadillac, where he began pumping the gas he had just paid for in the convenience store. He couldn't help but notice that the blonde in the SUV was looking his way. Rome couldn't blame her. He knew he was much smoother than the thick-necked guy she was stuck with. But the blonde was only a momentary distraction; something of far more concern was pulling up to the station.

It was a seriously tricked-out Chevy Camaro that had been converted into a patrol car, of all things. Rome assumed it was an impounded car that someone had thought would be more useful on the right side of the law. They obviously had their fun giving it a new paint job. Two highway patrol troopers sat inside as they pulled up to the gas tank behind the Cadillac.

Rome could see Vescera follow his eyes back to the troopers. Vescera remained cool on the surface, but seemed uneasy underneath. Rome hoped that he didn't look the same as he went back to pumping gas.

Now they would find out whether or not their pictures had made it out to the police yet. Rome knew that extra precautions had been taken to make sure that they remained anonymous; at least for a couple days. But he also knew that once Morgan had blown up the cop car, the rules of the game had changed. It was going to be difficult to keep a low profile. Especially when they were right under the nose of two cops.

As the officer in the passenger seat climbed out of the car, Rome chanced a glance into the big picture window of the convenience store. Bennett was at the register, buying an armload of junk food for the crew, since some of them hadn't had breakfast. Rome saw that Bennett was keeping an eye on the situation from his position. Angela was back on the other side of the small store. He could tell she was aware of the officer's presence as well.

Rome took stock of his surroundings. There was nothing to be concerned about. Other than the cashier, there was only one person in the store. Rome assumed that it was that guy's wife or girlfriend that was in the SUV beside them. As long as the troopers didn't raise any problems, and Morgan stayed in the bathroom, they'd be all right.

Somehow, Rome didn't think that Morgan was planning to spend all morning in the bathroom. He considered hurrying over and locking the guy inside, but there was no way Morgan would allow that to happen quietly.

The officer nodded toward the cashier, indicating that he'd like the pump turned on. Rome doubted the county reimbursed the station for the free gas, but this was just how things were done in small towns. The station that provided complimentary service received complimentary drive-bys throughout the day.

The officer—Brady according to his nametag—

turned to the gas tank, pulled out the nozzle, and started filling up the car. He glanced over at the Cadillac, giving it the once-over. Rome tried not to tense up. If they were going to get out of this, he was going to have to play the friendly traveler.

Officer Brady gave Rome a friendly nod hello, which Rome saw as an opportunity. He walked over to the officer in a neighborly fashion.

"Cadillac man, huh?" Brady asked.

"Sure," Rome replied as he checked out the cop car. "Interesting cruiser. It's got style. I like that."

"Even cops have to get around, right?" Brady replied brazenly. As if cops in the bigger cities could get away with flashy things like the Camaro.

"Look out, bad guys," Rome played along.

"Right," Brady said, bobbing his head.

Rome watched as Officer Brady's eyes went back to the convenience store. Inside, Bennett needlessly turned away from the cop, which made Rome a bit edgy. It was the definite look shared between Bennett and Vescera across the gas station parking lot that set Rome on edge. A good cop would be sensitive to guilty behavior like that. He just hoped that Brady wasn't a good cop.

"What happens there, stays there, huh?" Brady asked.

Rome didn't have a clue what the cop was talking about. "What?"

Brady nodded toward the Cadillac's bumper, where a sticker announcing the pleasures of Las Vegas was affixed.

"The Vegas sticker," he said. "On your bumper."

"Oh, yeah, yeah. It's my brother's car," Rome lied. "He used to live there. He just moved back last week." Rome could sense that the cop was picking up on something. His attitude had shifted from friendly to suspicious. Rome wondered exactly where this line of questioning was going, though.

"You go visit him much?" Brady asked.

"Couple times a year," Rome replied. Both men had forgotten about gassing up their cars.

"Me too," Brady said. "My mom lives in Vegas. I just love it there, especially downtown. You ever go over to the Olympus, see the fountains over there and all?"

Rome wasn't sure what the cop was playing at. The question was out of more than just friendly interest. Though he wasn't sure what his answer would tell the guy.

"Not since they tore it down," Rome said.

Officer Brady smiled as if he were satisfied with the response. Obviously the cop's hunch had proven wrong. Rome suspected the cop was digging around for suspicious behavior, like a needlessly made-up story. Anything that would support his curiosity over the obvious look between Bennett and Vescera could lead him down some path to know that something wasn't right.

Rome had managed to charm his way out of the situation. Thankfully, he had been to Vegas during March Madness to lay some friendly wagers and spent some time exploring the town. He allowed himself to relax. The cop had moved back to gassing up his car. He thought that everything would be all right.

Until he saw trouble walking his way with a strut in its step.

Morgan had finished up in the bathroom and was coming around from the side of the building. Rome saw him pause for a beat as he noticed the cop. Morgan kept walking, but he casually moved his hand behind his back. Rome wasn't sure if he was tucking in his shirt or reaching for his gun. He hoped for the former.

Morgan came over and greeted the cop. "How you doin'?"

The cop gave Morgan the once-over and nodded hello. Rome knew the concern on his face was visible, but he did his best to shield it from the cop. He tried to send Morgan a silent message to chill out, but the note obviously didn't make it in time.

Without a warning, Morgan pulled a gun from his waist and shot the officer in the head. From Rome's perspective, it was very unpleasant and even more unnecessary, as it set off a chain reaction of events that were seriously going to put a crimp in his plans for the rest of the day.

"Here we go!" Rome said.

The blond woman in the Navigator screamed.

Rome pulled his semiautomatic from inside his jacket and unloaded it into the tricked-out cruiser, aiming for Brady's partner. The cop shifted to reverse and returned fire as he threw the car backward in an effort to save himself.

It was time to kill or be killed.

As the car flew backward, the nozzle was ripped from the gas tank. It continued to pour gas onto the ground. Rome ignored the danger as he resumed firing into the car windshield. Apparently he had hit his mark because the car slammed into a pole and everything went silent.

Triton had been deciding between a chilled energy drink and a Yoo-Hoo when the gunshot and the scream pulled him out of his quiet morning.

"Kate!" he yelled, horrified that his home life seemed to be merging with his old work life. Gunfire and his wife simply did not mix.

Triton ran for the door, but before he could make it, the guy at the counter turned and slammed a fire extinguisher into his head. Triton flew back and slammed his head on the refrigerator door. His body wanted to black out, but he knew if that happened, Kate would be on her own. He fought to remain alert and regain control of his body.

Through blurred vision, he watched the store clerk throw his hands into the air.

"I didn't see anything," the clerk said. "It's cool. It's cool."

"It's *so* cool," the woman said. Regret did not stop her from firing two shots at the clerk. Triton could only focus on the blood that spurted onto the wall behind the guy. He did hear the body drop, taking out the cigarette rack as it fell.

Triton tried to force his body up, but the pain in his head was too intense. He knew Kate needed him, but there was nothing he could do. He managed to watch the man and woman flee the store before everything went black.

16

Rome was not happy.

There were two more dead cops in addition to the one from yesterday. Not to mention the kid at the jewelry store. He assumed there were two more dead men inside the gas station convenience store. Bennett and Angela were already leaving with their guns drawn. That left the current body count at six. And they hadn't even reached the drop point yet.

This was not what he'd had in mind when he noticed the gas tank was running on empty hardly ten minutes ago. It seemed as if incompetence reigned all around him. The next time he hired a vehicle guy, he'd make sure the idiot knew to get a car that was filled before they expected to use it in a getaway.

At least the woman had stopped screaming for the moment. He knew it wasn't likely that was going to last for long. Especially when she realized her traveling companion wasn't coming out of the store. On the other hand, if she started screaming again, he knew *that* wouldn't last long either.

Morgan was heading for the woman with his gun drawn. As far as Rome could tell, she was the only witness left. Rome could see her going for the driver's side, but it was too late. Morgan was already there.

The woman pulled back to the passenger's side and was surprised to find Vescera had already thrown open the Navigator and was grabbing at her.

With the situation seemingly under control, Rome prepared to depart. Someone was bound to stumble across this scene soon enough. They weren't exactly on a major highway, but it was busy enough.

A quick check of the Cadillac stopped him. The cop's wild shots had managed to blow out one of the back tires. The car wasn't going anywhere on that wheel, and they didn't have the luxury of time to change it.

"The truck!" Rome called out to his crew.

As he ran over to the Navigator, Vescera yanked the blonde out the side door.

"No! Take her!" Rome yelled. "A hostage could come in handy."

Bennett climbed into the far backseat as Vescera shoved the woman into the middle row. Meanwhile, Angela was heading around the SUV to the passenger side.

Even though he knew there wasn't time, Rome grabbed Morgan as he started to get in the back too.

"Morgan," Rome asked in a forcedly pleasant tone, "why'd you do that?"

"I'm not exactly sure," Morgan replied, looking honestly confused by his own actions. "I think it may have been all that coffee I drank."

Rome watched as Morgan hopped into the back on the SUV. Rome wasn't sure if having a lunatic on his team was a good thing or a bad thing. On the positive side, it made Rome look positively sane by comparison.

Rome slammed the door shut, then hopped in the driver's seat. He turned to see Angela beside him, meeting him with an exasperated look. Rome just shrugged in a "What can you do?" kind of way as he started the engine.

"You want to what?" the voice asked with measured calmness.

It took John a moment to focus on his surroundings. He was in his parents' house. In the sitting room. He used to call it the Gallery Room because it always looked like one of those rooms that were re-created in art galleries using furniture from long-dead civilizations. The kinds of rooms that were roped off so that no one could enter. His family's sitting room looked very much like a roped-off room.

John could tell his father was angry by the fact that he had lost all emotion in his voice. Not that Jonathan Triton Sr. had much emotion in his voice to begin with. It was a fine line, but John knew it well. If there was anyone who could remove even the last trace of emotion from his father's voice, it was John Jr.

"I want to join the Marines," John said firmly. "I *have* joined the Marines."

For a brief moment, John saw an actual emotion cross his father's face. It was gone as quickly as it had come, but John recognized it immediately. It was rage.

Even at the age of eighteen John knew rage. He felt it all the time on the football field. He wasn't sure exactly where it came from. Certainly his parents never experienced rage. It was like John had gotten all the emotion in the family. His father had the brains. His mother had the social skills. They were always quick to remind John of what he lacked.

"We shall see about that," his father said coolly.

"It's done," John said. "I start training the week after graduation."

"It is most certainly *not* done," his father said. "I can see to that."

"You can't—"

"Yes," his father said. "I can."

"You *won't*," John said, gathering every ounce of strength that he had. John had never stood up to his father before. It simply wasn't done in his house. At least, he hadn't done it so boldly before. Yet everything John had done in his life was in one way or other to make his father angry. Not that his father ever got angry.

"Fine," Jonathan said, as if he was giving in. He never argued with his family. They weren't worth his time. "In one week you will pack your bags and join the Marines. However, when you go on leave, please do not bother coming home for a visit. And when you . . . what is the term? Wash out? Do not come to me looking for help."

Without another word, Jonathan Triton turned and left the sitting room. He went into his home office, carefully shutting the door behind him so he would be free to conduct his business without being interrupted.

John slumped into the nearest chair. The saddest part about that conversation—if he could call it that—was that it happened exactly as John had imagined it would. He had learned early on that his father's expectations were ridiculous. Jonathan Triton strived for the best, and he expected no less from his son. But John knew that no matter what he did, he would never be the best in his father's eyes. His grades certainly weren't the best. His social skills were severely lacking. Even if they had been at top form, his father would find something else to be disappointed in. Even when John was named All-State in football, his father could only say, "But it's football. It's not like it's going to help him in life."

Early on, John decided that he wasn't even going to try to make his father proud. The first blow came when John convinced his mother to send him to the local public school. He had used his father's own standing in the community against his parents by convincing his mom that there was no better way to show that his father supported his town by not sending his son to the private school an hour's bus ride away, sending him to the local public school instead. Then John worked with his choice of friends. Sure, Joe was a great guy, but John often wondered if he ever would have sat down next to the guy on the first day of school if he hadn't been exactly the type of person Jonathan would have gone out of his way to avoid.

The problem with not caring about disappointing his dad was that John was afraid of disappointing himself. He never really strived for anything. Sure, some considered his performance on the football field impressive, but John knew there were dozens of other guys in the state that played far better than him.

But, joining—and being a part of—the Marines was different. That was something he knew he could excel at to the core of his being. He wasn't sure why he knew that. He had always been good in scouts. And Lord knew he had years of tight discipline at home to fall back on. But he had never even considered the Marines until they came recruiting at school. From the moment the Marine, in his cleanly pressed uniform, handed John the brochure, he knew right down to his soul that it was his calling.

He was going to be a Marine.

Light slowly filtered through Triton's eyes. His senses began to reawaken. As nice as it felt to know he wasn't actually dead, it was disconcerting to know that he *felt* like he was. His head hurt. His chest ached. It took him a moment to realize he wasn't in a desert wearing fatigues. He was in a gas station in South Carolina, dressed in civvies. This kind of thing wasn't supposed to happen here.

He still couldn't move, and he wasn't sure what *had* happened. It seemed like a robbery, but he didn't remember anyone asking the clerk for cash before they killed him. Then he remembered that the shooting had started outside the store. And there were cops involved. And Kate was . . .

Kate!

Triton's eyes popped open. He was still in pain, but it didn't matter. He had to find Kate.

Slowly, and with difficulty, he managed to pull himself up off the ground. The clerk was dead on the floor. Cigarettes were spilled around him, but the register was still closed. Otherwise, there was nothing to indicate that anything had happened.

The scene outside the store was a different story.

A police car had slammed into a pole that had come crashing down on it. An officer was down by the gas tanks. It looked like he was in a puddle of gasoline.

The sound of screeching tires pulled Triton's mind back into focus. The man he had passed when entering the store was behind the wheel of the Navigator. *His* Navigator. The SUV was currently peeling out of the station. He could see Kate struggling in the back seat.

The woman who'd shot the clerk was leaning out of the passenger window. She sprayed the ground with gunfire from a semiautomatic. Triton watched as the bullets cut a path to the puddle of gasoline.

As the Navigator pulled away, the puddle went up in flames that quickly spread to the gas pumps. The pumps blew in a huge explosion, instantly turning the gas station into an inferno.

The explosion blew out the store windows and sent Triton flying backward for the second time in a span of only a few minutes. He slammed back into the refrigerators, but managed to remain conscious as glass and debris fell around him.

Through the wall of flame, he thought he could see

Kate disappearing as the SUV pulled onto the highway. She looked horrified. He could understand why. From her perspective it must have looked like she was watching her husband die. For a passing moment, Triton thought she very well could have been if Triton didn't move quickly.

The mini-mart was totally engulfed in flames. It was a roaring firestorm that smelled of gasoline, smoke, and burning food products. He could hear the roof buckling and beams snapping. Suddenly, part of the burning roof came collapsing in on him. His body was buried in debris.

For a moment, there was only silence. And darkness. But Triton knew that he was still conscious. Through the silence he heard a sharp, piercing sound. In his mind, all he could see was Kate.

Like a phoenix rising from the flames, Triton slowly emerged from the debris that had fallen on top of him. The piercing sound was a ringing in his ears. It was already beginning to fade as he struggled to his feet, dazed, disoriented, and bloody.

He once again could see out past the smoke and haze. The Navigator was heading down the highway. It was already too far for him to see Kate in the window, but he knew she was in there. The murderers had taken her hostage. Probably for protection when the police caught up with them. But Triton couldn't wait for the police to get around to finding her. He knew that she was about to disappear from his life for good if he didn't stop them on his own.

* * *

Adrenaline and rage forced Triton through the burning store and falling debris as he made his way through the smashed glass doors and to the outside. It was just as hot outside with the burning tanks still lit, but at least the air was fresher.

He surveyed the destruction. All that was left aside from the burning tanks was a smoked-out Cadillac and a slightly damaged police cruiser with what looked to be a dead policeman inside. As Triton ran for the cruiser, the Cadillac exploded, throwing a wave of heat at Triton, but he managed to stay on his feet.

As Triton reached the car, he saw that the cop inside was still alive. Barely.

Triton pulled his dog tags out from his shirt and flashed them in front of the dazed officer. "I'm a Marine. I'll call for help."

He carefully pulled the officer from the damaged car. The cop's nametag read "Effren." Triton could make out a Kevlar vest poking out of the holes in Effren's bullet-ridden shirt. Even though Effren looked like he wasn't suffering any fatal wounds, he was bleeding from the shoulder and collarbone. He would be no help in getting Kate back.

"I gotta take your car," Triton told the dazed officer. "They have my wife."

The cop was too out of it to protest, which was just as well. Triton wouldn't have heard him. His heart was pounding too loudly in his own ears. It replaced the ringing, which was totally gone.

Triton grabbed the cop's revolver and ammo from the man's belt. He jumped into the car—surprised to find it was a tricked-out Camaro—and drove off. His mind was focused on a singular objective. Saving Kate.

Triton floored it, pulling onto the blacktop. He was driving hard, with his heart still pounding in his chest. The killing rage that had possessed him in Afghanistan—that he had barely even tapped into the day before with "The Drake"—took over more intensely than it ever had before.

In battle, he was only concerned with the safety of his men and himself. This was different. This was his wife. If he had been known to proceed recklessly before, it was nothing compared to what he was willing to do today.

He snatched up the CB and keyed the mike. "Highway patrol . . . This is John Triton. You've got officers down at Manze's Gas Station. Multiple assailants. Four men, one woman. Heading southbound on I-95. They're in a black Navigator, and they have a hostage. My wife."

As Triton completed the transmission, he could finally see the Navigator up ahead in the distance. It was moving quickly, but Triton knew he could overtake them in the cruiser.

The chase was on.

Sergeant John Triton (John Cena) disobeys orders to rescue fellow Marines taken captive by an Al Qaeda militant group.

ABOVE
Three Special Forces Marines (Remi Broadway, Steve Harman, Damien Bryson) await their execution at the hands of Al Qaeda militants.

RIGHT
On a military base in Stuttgart, Germany, Colonel Braun (Robert Coleby) regrettably informs Triton that he has been discharged from the United States Marine Corps.

RIGHT
Angela's beauty and brains make her a lethal asset in Rome's crew.

BELOW
Rome and Triton engage in a final, desperate battle within a burning shoreline oil depot.

Triton dashes for the nearest exit as the fishing lodge erupts into flames.

With Triton still hot on their tails, Angela and Rome force Kate along at gunpoint while trying to escape the fishing lodge.

En route to a drop point meeting with his silent partner, Rome leads his gang and captive deep into South Carolina woodland.

At a stand-off in the lodge, Triton bolts toward Detective Van Buren (Jerome Ehlers.)

ABOVE
Leaving Triton's now-useless Navigator behind, Angela (Abigail Bianca), Bennett (Manu Bennett), Morgan (Anthony Ray Parker), and Vescera (Damon Gibson) dread the upcoming trek through the swampland.

RIGHT
Running through the swamps of South Carolina, nothing will stop Triton from saving his wife.

OPPOSITE PAGE
Holding Kate hostage, Angela, Morgan, and Bennett await Rome's next move.

Rome's (Robert Patrick) armed robbery in the diamond district turns deadly when police try to intervene.

Triton and his loving wife Kate (Kelly Carlson) celebrate his first night back home.

17

Kate could barely hold back her tears. This kind of thing wasn't supposed to happen. Not here. John was finally home, safe and sound. No more war. No more life-and-death missions. It was almost cruel. For her to spend so much time worrying about John when he was overseas, only to experience the true horror after he returned home.

She refused to believe he was gone. Things like this didn't happen. They just didn't happen. Part of her knew she was in denial, but that didn't matter. If she didn't accept what she had just seen, she was perfectly fine allowing herself to believe it had never occurred. She sat, steel-jawed, with a gun held to her head, refusing to cry or show any sign of fear.

The woman—someone had called her Angela—was riffling through the glove compartment. Kate went from numb to angry in a flash. She didn't know why *that*—after all that she had just witnessed in the space of a few minutes—really got to her. The invasion of privacy seemed almost more personal.

Angela had pulled out Kate's base parking pass and assorted other junk.

"Kate Triton," Angela read off the pass, shooting a glance back at her. "Married to John Triton . . . wait . . . my mistake, *Sergeant* John Triton." She looked at the driver. "She married a Marine. How sweet."

Kate was tempted to punch the bitch, but she knew she'd never get away with it surrounded by the rest of the goons.

Angela turned to her. "What did you marry him for? The benefits?"

"Well, if Triton was the redneck in the store back there," the guy behind Kate said—she thought his name was Bennett—"he's dead."

That was all Kate needed to hear; someone putting her fears into words. Screw logic. To hell with denial. She knew she'd never get the guy behind her, so she lunged at the woman in the front seat.

Unfortunately, the guy in the back—Bennett—yanked Kate back into her own seat by her hair. The sharp pain was nothing compared to the anguish in her heart. She barely noticed when he released her hair and held another gun to her head.

"Settle down," he said.

Kate seethed, but tried to calm herself. Getting killed would do no good. She just needed to wait things out until they stopped. John hadn't had the chance to gas up the SUV before all hell broke loose, so they couldn't be going all that far. She knew her kidnappers would never let her go willingly, but she believed that she could escape them at some point. She had to believe it. Or else, with John gone, she had nothing else to live for.

If only she knew why they needed her. What happened at the gas station was a bit over the top for a simple mini-mart robbery. Clearly they had been involved in something big enough that it justified—to them—killing cops. If only she had watched the news last night, she might have had an idea. But she had been so set on avoiding any stories about John's horrible day that she had made sure the television was firmly off at eleven.

"You have got to be kidding me!" the driver, Rome, said, pulling her out of her wonderings.

Kate looked up and saw that his eyes were locked on the rearview mirror. She had hoped that help would come. The explosions at the gas station certainly wouldn't have gone unnoticed. She just didn't expect it to arrive so quickly. Oddly, she didn't hear any sirens.

She turned back, as everyone else in the SUV did, and was thrilled to see a police car blazing toward them. The first thing she noticed about it was that it was a sporty ride, almost exactly like the one that had pulled up at the gas station. *That's weird.* It seemed unlikely that the entire highway patrol drove such expensive sports cars.

As the squad car closed the distance, Kate could see that it was pretty banged up, like the one at the gas station had been. Then she realized it was the same car. Once that thought set in, she strained a bit harder to see into the car, and what she saw set her heart into overdrive. There wasn't a cop at the wheel. It was John. He was alive, and he was going to save her.

Kate almost felt sorry for her captors. There was no way they were prepared to deal with the kind of training John possessed. She had certainly heard stories of his less classified exploits. She was almost excited to see him in action. Kate considered using the distraction to make a move for one of the guys' guns, but that would have still left four weapons aimed at her. She decided to bide her time and wait for a better opening.

"Get ready," Rome said as the cruiser came up fast on them.

Kate fastened her seat belt, preparing for the worst. Everyone else in the SUV raised their weapons.

"You must be really somethin', girl," the black guy said to her. "If somebody took my woman, I'd just wave good-bye. But those are my issues—"

Kate just added that one to the long list of issues she suspected the psychopath had locked in his pathetic excuse for a brain.

"Shoot him!" Rome yelled.

Triton was bearing down on the Navigator. The huge SUV filled his field of vision. He could see Kate moving inside. Her blond hair was like a beacon in the shadowy interior of the vehicle. She was still alive.

With renewed determination, he pressed the accelerator to the floor. The car bucked forward as it advanced. He took in the situation, trying to develop the perfect plan to save his wife and lay waste to her kidnappers. Triton had no clue what these people were running from, or what they had done, but he was certain that they could not possibly be prepared to handle what he was about to throw at them.

Suddenly, the Navigator's back window exploded with gunfire as the squad car's own windshield was riddled with bullets.

Triton stayed low as shotgun blasts sparked around him. He keyed the radio, with the mike still in his hand. "This is John Triton. Is anybody there?"

The radio was dead. One of the shots had taken out the antenna. Or maybe it had been gone since the gas station. Triton wasn't sure. He hadn't received any response since he'd first tried using it.

He threw the mike down on to the floor as he clasped the steering wheel with both hands. It was going to take some serious driving to stop the SUV. Luckily, he had a hell of a lot of training behind him in that particular area. Racing over a paved highway was nothing compared to zipping through the desert trying to catch a terrorist to prevent him from blowing up a manned checkpoint.

Bullets tore into the black-and-white, decimating what was left of the windshield.

Triton drove with his head down, presenting as small a target as he could, considering his size. A barrage of rounds sailed through the empty windshield frame, tearing apart the seats and the car interior. He could feel one of the bullets that had embedded itself in the headrest, somehow missing the top of his skull by mere fractions of an inch. Triton kept his foot on the accelerator, glancing up only long enough to make sure he was still on the Navigator's tail.

He pulled the cop's gun out of his waistband. It almost felt odd to have a weapon in his hand again. He really thought that that part of his life had ended. This trip was supposed to be about starting over with Kate. He was not about to let some worthless scumbags take Kate from him too.

Triton took another peek above the dash to return fire. All he heard was the repeated click-click-click of an empty clip. Thinking back to what happened at the station, Triton realized that the cop had probably unloaded everything on the Caddy driver when he'd come under attack. Triton cursed himself for not checking the weapon's status sooner. He wasn't thinking clearly because they had his wife, but that was no excuse. Years of training had prepared him for a situation like this—but no amount of training could prepare him for the reality of his wife being involved.

Triton reached into his pocket to pull out the ammo he had taken from the cop. He desperately tried to reload as he split his attention between loading the gun and pulling up even with the SUV.

"Will somebody shoot this guy?" Rome said calmly as he looked out the rearview and saw that Sergeant John Triton was still approaching. With the kind of day Rome was having, it figured they'd take the wife of a Marine. If only it had been some pipsqueak IT guy who would have just called it in and waited for the police to do their jobs for him. No, they *had* to get a human tank.

Morgan was the only one still firing. Rome assumed that the rest were trying to gain their bearings. There was no use wasting bullets on a guy that refused to die. Of course, nobody was gonna tell that to Morgan.

"This guy must have a death wish," Bennett said as he took aim again.

Morgan laughed a crazy laugh that was somehow fitting for the man. "Then I'm the Make-a-Wish Foundation up in this mutha—"

Gunfire erupted before he could finish the sentence as Angela, Vescera, and Bennett also emptied their weapons, following Morgan's lead.

And yet, Rome noted, *the Marine still isn't dead.*

Triton was trying to pull up beside the SUV, but Rome wasn't about to let that happen. He swung the Navigator over and rammed the side of the police car as the crew reloaded and resumed firing.

From his spot behind the wheel, Rome saw that Triton had been reloading as well, but lost his gun when Rome knocked the Navigator into him. Bullets had flown all over the passenger seat. At least something was going right, finally. His guys certainly hadn't managed to do any real damage to Triton yet.

"Son of a bitch won't quit," Angela yelled over the gunfire.

There was another pause in the gunfire. It lasted

only a moment before it was on again, just as vicious as before.

Triton tried to reach for his gun, but he couldn't get it. The smack from the Navigator had knocked it out of his hand and onto the floor in the passenger-seat well. He slowed the car slightly as he reached for the weapon, dropping back behind his SUV again. He doubted that his insurance would cover what it was going through at the moment.

He continued to dodge the gunfire, but the tricked-out cop car could only take so much. The hood of the police car was ripped off in the assault. It went up, blinding him for a moment before coming loose and flipping up and over the car.

As Triton weaved behind the Navigator, he slammed through a sign warning, "Road Construction Ahead." The irony of it was that at the moment, it was the construction workers who needed a warning. Triton considered looking for the siren controls, but figured it would probably be useless to activate them. If the construction workers couldn't hear the two cars screeching down the highway with bullets flying, it was their own damn fault if they didn't get out of the way.

A road worker with a stop sign ineffectively—and idiotically—tried to wave off the Navigator and the police car, warning them to slow down. If he had been paying any attention to the state of either vehicle, he would have realized it was a pointless endeavor. They blew past the worker, sending orange cones flying in every direction.

About a hundred yards up ahead of the SUV, Triton could see a huge ditch-digger in the path. It was getting closer with every passing millisecond as they raced over the torn-up road. The Navigator was on a collision course. He hoped that Kate had her seat belt on because things were about to get ugly . . . *uglier*.

The driver of his stolen SUV saw the heavy machinery too. He hit the brakes, slowing the SUV and swinging it to the side. The rear of the SUV slammed back into the police car, sending Triton veering off the road, heading directly for the ditch-digger's hanging scoop.

Triton swerved in an attempt to miss the scoop, but the obviously panicked driver of the ditch-digger reacted as well, sending the scoop in the opposite direction and straight into Triton's path again. Triton tried to react in a split second and maneuver on a dime, but that was truly impossible in the battered car. It was too late.

The former Marine kept his foot on the gas as he threw his body to the side and ducked onto the passenger's seat. The two-ton scoop smashed into what was left of the windshield, tearing the entire roof off of the police car. Metal crunched under metal with resounding force as the tricked-out Camaro became a convertible. The top of the car was gone, torn off like the lid of a soup can and discarded just the same.

* * *

Kate had experienced a whole slew of emotions within the last few seconds. Fear was topmost among them. Fear for herself, yes, but mostly fear for John. She was overjoyed when she saw his head pop back up in the police car after the horror of watching the roof being wrenched away.

John's eyes were focused, his drive relentless. She could see his face was set with a look that she had never seen before. No matter how many stories he had told of battle, this was a side of John she had never understood. But now, seeing him in action helped her to understand him just a little better. When they got out of this, she knew it was going to be even harder to help him find his way in the civilian world. At least the thought of helping him gave her something to look forward to.

It also helped build her resolve. If John could go through all this to save her, then damned if she was just going to sit idly by, waiting for him. Kate knew she had her own form of inner strength. It was time for her to tap into the well.

"He's still coming!" Angela yelled.

Kate could see the look of shock and amazement on all of their faces. She had been proud of her husband before, but now she was in awe.

Emboldened by John's courage and drive, Kate slipped her seatbelt off, dove forward and grabbed Rome by the head. At the very least, she was hoping to give John an opening that he could exploit. The SUV swerved as Rome was forced to twist the steering wheel hard to the right as she pulled him away.

Kate was thrown off balance by the move, and Vescera was able to yank her back into her seat. But the damage had been done. She had set them on a different path. It was a small victory, and she would take what she could get.

Rome was forced to veer off the road to avoid colliding with a tree. The SUV blasted through a weather-ravaged sign that Kate barely had the time to read. Relief filled her at what she had seen. The sign had read: "Dead End." They would have to stop the SUV. Then John would have a chance to take them out.

She hoped that this would, in fact, be the end. Though a shiver ran down her spine; she feared who would wind up dead.

Triton swung up behind the wheel of the now topless police car. He was able to see Kate attacking the driver of the SUV. He beamed with pride in his wife and her refusal to be a helpless victim. Then he felt a renewed sense of rage as he saw her roughly pulled back into her seat.

He slammed on the squad car's brakes as the SUV veered off the highway and careened down a narrow path through dense swampland. Swinging the car around in a hard skid, he continued the pursuit. Tires squealed as he stomped on the gas and took the car off-road and down the narrow path where the Navigator had disappeared.

The trees were thick around the path, which made

it harder to see. Branches brushed past the open-air car as Triton struggled to keep it on the narrow road. He fought with the steering wheel as the police car bounced and slid through the underbrush. Even on its best day, the car wasn't built for off-roading. And this was far from the car's best day.

Up ahead, the Navigator skidded to a halt, slipping through the dirt and mud toward a riverbank. Even though the SUV was built for terrain like this, it wasn't often that Kate had taken it through the swamps on her days off. Triton braced himself for the showdown as he continued to barrel through the trees.

The woman on the passenger side hung out the window and fired on Triton with her twin Colts. Another guy leaned out the tailgate, firing a Protecta. He wondered if they were ever going to run out of bullets.

The fusillade of bullets slammed into the police car's exposed engine, igniting oil lines and setting off an explosion in the front of the car. Triton ducked a fireball that raged over the body of the car. When he came back up he realized that he was heading straight for the Navigator. There was no time to stop on the wet mud. In a moment, he'd be inside the SUV, possibly killing the woman he was rushing to save in the process.

Triton could not weave fast enough to save both himself and Kate. He yanked the wheel to the right. The police car clipped a fallen tree along the side of the dirt road and was sent flying into the air, rolling over left to right.

Everything seemed to be happening in slow motion as Triton heard massive weapons fire beneath him. The police car was flying right over the Navigator. Kate's kidnappers were firing at the car's undercarriage as it somersaulted overhead.

An army of bullets slammed and sliced into the police car, ripping into the undercarriage and puncturing the fuel tank. The cruiser exploded in midair. Triton was ejected from the burning car in a cloud of fire.

Triton and the burning car spiraled down separately, plunging into the swampy river.

Kate's body went numb as she watched the car's chassis sink down into the water. Bubbles churned from the sunken debris as she clung onto the dim hope that some of that was air from John's breath. Flames were burning on the surface of the water.

The Navigator sat at the river's muddy bank, battered and beaten, much like Kate felt. She couldn't accept getting John back again only to lose him so quickly.

The crew climbed out of the Navigator. Kate was numb and couldn't move, but Morgan dragged her out with him. She could only stare at the water where John had disappeared. She was emotionally spent. Devastated.

"John!" she screamed before turning on Rome and his crew. "You bastards! You murdering sons of bitches!"

Kate thrashed wildly as she wailed in grief. Her fists battered Rome, Bennett, and anyone else within striking distance. She didn't care that she was risking her life by attacking them. With John gone, she had nothing left to live for.

As she flailed at Rome, she was even more enraged that he was taking no more notice of her than he would have a bothersome fly. As if her grief and the loss of a human life meant nothing to them, which, she supposed, it didn't.

"Somebody shut her up," Rome said calmly.

Angela grabbed Kate and put a gun to her head, stopping Kate in her tracks. The anger and hurt were still there, but Kate knew she had to regain control. John wouldn't have wanted her to die out here. He hadn't given up his life so she would throw hers away so quickly.

But her life was in Angela's hands now. Kate heard the click of the hammer cocking as Angela prepared to fire her gun. Her blood ran cold.

"Wait," Rome said, casually holding up his hand. "We might still need an insurance policy."

Kate looked back down the road they had taken. It was barely a road—almost impossible to see from the highway. No one was coming at the moment, but she knew that they couldn't just go unnoticed, trashing a construction site and blowing up a police car after speeding away from an exploding gas station. Someone would be coming soon. All she had to do was hold out until then. When she was saved, she'd see these murderers rot in jail . . . or worse. Unsurprisingly, she had quickly rethought her opinion of the death penalty. These jackasses would pay. Then she'd give her husband a proper funeral.

Tears stung her eyes as she slowly accepted that she was now alone. Kate knew she still had the strength that her husband had given her to carry through. It would have to be enough. She'd see herself out of this ordeal and maybe take one or two of the bastards out in the meantime.

Kate went limp as Angela grabbed a rope from the SUV and bound her hands. She'd have another chance. She'd see to that.

In the meantime, she remained silent, considering her limited means of escape despite being numb with grief. Her eyes gazed out hopelessly at the flaming river as her mind kept going back to John.

18

Rome waited while Vescera checked under the SUV. Things were not looking good. Somewhere along the way this simple robbery had gone horribly awry. He knew much of the fault was with Morgan and his rather unenlightened way of dealing with the law. Of course, Rome couldn't totally blame the guy. He had been aware of that particular shortcoming when he hired Morgan onto the team. In a way, it was kind of Rome's fault that Morgan felt pushed to the point where he had to keep killing cops.

That had to be it. Rome couldn't think of any other reason why he hadn't plugged Morgan's ass any earlier. Somehow Rome felt responsible for the guy. Morgan was almost childlike in the way he looked at the world. There was something about the man that made Rome just want to look after him. Rome thought it was a shame that Morgan probably wouldn't make it through the day. Especially if he kept acting up like he had been.

"Front axle's history," Vescera said as he slid out from under the SUV. "We're not going anywhere in this thing."

"Ah, you figure that out all by yourself?" Morgan asked.

Once again, Rome couldn't blame the guy. It seemed pretty obvious that the damn Navigator was well out of commission. But it was good to have the confirmation. Better than trekking through the swamp for no reason.

"Yeah, actually, I did," Vescera said, heating up. "You know what else I figured out?"

"What's that?" Morgan asked, responding in temper to Vescera.

"You're a trigger-happy nut job that belongs in a cage," Vescera yelled. "With all the other animals."

The words cut deep into Morgan, as far as Rome could tell. Mind you, they were true, but Vescera didn't have to go saying that in front of everyone. Rome suspected that Morgan's problems with law enforcement were about to spill over to issues with the crew. It happened a bit faster than Rome had expected.

Morgan threw himself at Vescera, punching and kicking with reckless abandon. Rome didn't doubt that Morgan could do some serious damage if his heart was in it, but it just seemed like he was blowing off some steam. Bennett tried to pull the two men apart, getting hold of Morgan and keeping him from killing the man who brought him onto the crew in the first place. As Morgan continued to rage, it seemed that Vescera was finding the entire thing particularly amusing.

Rome, however, was not.

He fired two shots into the air, figuring it wouldn't

draw any more attention than the exploding cop car had. The scuffle stopped instantly. Rome was done with this bullshit. His gun was in hand, and his good humor was gone. It wasn't a good combination.

"All right," he said, addressing Morgan and Vescera, "we are monumentally screwed here, and the last thing I need to worry about is the two of you bickering like a couple of little girls"—he turned to the women—"no offense, ladies."

Rome stepped up to the two men. "So, as of right now, it's over. We clear? Because if we're not, I give you my word, I will absolutely shoot you myself."

Morgan and Vescera heard what Rome was saying, and they knew that he meant it. They both backed down immediately.

Rome was afraid that his team was coming apart at the seams. He needed to hold them together. They were stuck at the edge of the swamp with no means of getting out except on foot. And there were definitely cops on the way soon. At least they had a hostage to keep things balanced a bit more in their favor.

"So what now?" Bennett asked, stepping forward.

It was a stupid question, but Rome figured someone would ask it. At least it wasn't Angela.

"Well, we have a couple options," he said, failing to keep the condescension out of his voice. "We could, A, stay here and continuing trying to kill each other, but then nobody gets paid and somebody gets dead. Or we could, B, get out of this swamp, make the drop, and collect our money." He paused for effect. "Now,

maybe it's just greed talking, but I'm going with B."
He looked questioningly at the others.

"I say we move fast," Bennett said, obviously going
with plan B as well. "Half the state must have seen that
blast back there." Bennett looked around, surveying
the situation. "If we go downstream through the
swamp, we're bound to find something."

Rome looked over the swamp again. He could tell
his crew was doing the same. Rome, for one, hadn't
dressed for traveling through swampland today, but he
saw little other choice in the matter. It would be a difficult trek, but he knew his crew was fueled by the
same desire he had for pursuing option B.

"Through there?" Morgan said, giving voice to
everyone's skepticism.

"Look, he's right," Rome said. "The trees hide us
from the air, and the swamp will slow the cops down.
Let's go."

It was decision time for the crew, but Rome knew
something they didn't. He had already made the
choice for each of them. Either they went with him
and found a way out of the swamp, or they didn't. And
if they didn't, they weren't getting out of the swamp
at all.

"And what about our little 'insurance policy' here?"
Angela asked, shoving Kate.

"Go to hell," Kate said.

Angela pistol-whipped the hostage, knocking her
out cold.

"Aw, see. Why did you do that?" Rome asked. He

kind of admired Kate's spunk. Then again, the last thing he needed was any additional spunk at the moment. But he had other reasons for being bothered by Angela's rash action. "Now Morgan's got to carry her."

That information caught Morgan off guard, and he didn't seem to like it much. "Morgan's got to do what?"

Rome looked pointedly at Morgan, daring him to say something. He had put up with Morgan's rash actions to this point, but forgiveness only went so far. Morgan was going to carry Kate, or somebody would be carrying *him*, in a nice wooden box.

Rome gestured to Kate's body, forcing Morgan to back down and pick her up, throwing her over his shoulder.

"Keep your eyes open for crocs," Vescera said, with a glance to the swamp.

"What's the matter with you?" Bennett scoffed. "There're no crocodiles in South Carolina."

Rome chose not to comment as they headed downstream.

Triton tried to calm himself and allow his body to relax. He knew that reducing the level of stress on his body was the only way he was going to conserve oxygen. He could already feel a tightening in his lungs as his body warned him that he was running out of air. He was only a couple feet from the water's surface, but he could not reach it.

The explosion had blown Triton out of the car, into the relative safety of the river. He had smacked hard into the surface of the water before sinking to the depths below. Then, in a strange twist of irony or fate or something, the car came crashing down on top of him again. It was slowed due to the water, so it did no real damage as it landed on him, but his leg was caught between the waterlogged frame and a rock. He wasn't going anywhere for the moment.

Triton tugged at his leg, but it was locked in tightly. He needed to get free, but he couldn't damage the leg in the process. Once he was back on the surface, Kate would need him to be in one piece for her. Triton knew he was never going to lift the car off himself. Sure, he could call upon every ounce of strength he had in reserve and try to use the natural buoyancy of the water to help move the car, but that would just waste the little breath he had left. Since going up wouldn't work, it was time to go down.

Triton clawed at the soft mud beneath his leg. If he could get enough clearance, he could slide his foot out. Underwater, this was a difficult task because every time he pushed the mud aside, it just flowed back into the resulting hole. But Triton was persistent. He knew that eventually he would win against the wet earth. What he hadn't expected was to make some headway with the stone.

As Triton dug into the ground, he could feel the rock that was pressed up against his leg begin to shift. Changing tack, he slid his arm around and dug out the other side of the rock. All he needed was another inch, and he'd be clear.

His lungs were tightening as the last bits of oxygen were expelled. It wouldn't be long before he passed out and his body's involuntary systems took over. His mouth would open and suck in water, hoping to get some air. His lungs would flood, and he would drown.

But that was not going to happen. He would not allow it to happen. The rock began to give way. It slid far enough for Triton to turn his ankle and slide out from under the decimated squad car. Racing to the surface, Triton didn't care if he came up out of the water with five guns aimed at him. He needed air.

Triton popped up out of the surface of the river through a break in the flames. His lungs were bursting as he gasped for much-needed oxygen. He was alive and possessing newfound determination that he would not let Kate down.

Once he was breathing regularly, Triton took stock of the situation. The shoreline was empty. He didn't know what direction Kate's kidnappers had taken her. Flames continued to consume the debris floating around him.

Pulling himself out of the water, Triton took off his yellow-checked shirt, dropping it to the ground. His wet T-shirt clung to his body, but he felt pounds lighter without the wet button-down shirt pulling on him. Triton dropped to his knees when he was fully out of the water. There wasn't much time to rest, but he needed to take a moment. He had been through much more physical stress before, but nothing in his past had prepared him for the emotional drain he was experiencing.

Triton slid his body onto a rock so he could sit and think about his next move. He was going to rescue Kate, no matter what it took. He'd kill anyone that got in his way. He'd sacrifice his own life for hers. He swore that to himself, to Kate, and to the U.S. Marine Corps.

19

Detective Van Buren surveyed the crime scene at the gas station. It was kind of how he imagined downtown Baghdad looked on a bad day. A burned car sat beside the remains of the gas pumps. All of the glass windows in the mini-mart had been blown out. Parts of the building were still smoldering. Shattered glass and bullet holes littered the area.

That was just the cosmetic stuff. Two dead bodies and one officer fighting for his life were the serious parts. One of the dead was a cop. That meant another cop had died in the line, bringing the number to two in as many days. The county had already gone on high alert.

Fire trucks, squad cars, and a couple coroner vehicles filled the station. All had their dome lights flashing. The people from those vehicles were going over the station with a fine-toothed comb, looking for anything that could be of use in the investigation. CSIs were already giving the burned-out car the once-over, hoping to salvage some prints from the vehicle. Highway patrol had already cordoned off the crime scene and blocked the highway. No one was getting near the station until they knew exactly what happened.

Van Buren was already halfway to figuring it out.

"One deceased officer there," Officer Kelley reported, pointing to the remains of the gas pumps. He led the detective along a vehicle's skid marks in the driveway. "Another found seriously wounded here."

"And the guy who called it in?" Van Buren asked.

"John Triton, ex-Marine," the officer said with an impressed tone. Van Buren knew the officer would have already pulled up the man's record. "He's for real."

The detective considered the obvious. "From his description of the perps, sounds like the crew who hit that diamond store in town yesterday." That much was obvious as far as Van Buren was concerned. The real question was why they did it. Why they'd killed another cop. "Roadblocks up?"

"Yes, sir."

"Pull the bridges?"

"Yes, sir. Choppers and search teams are on the way."

Van Buren wasn't surprised. The city and state would be calling out the heavy artillery for this one. Two cops dead, one that could go either way. What could have been a simple robbery had just turned into a statewide manhunt. He knew without a doubt that he was no longer in charge of the investigation. With the criminals heading down the highway and presumably out of state, it was going to wind up with the FBI eventually. Until then, he was going to do all that he could to make sure he was in control until someone forced him to stop. He probably still had a few hours of work before the feds started getting in his way.

Van Buren walked with Officer Kelley into the store past where the clerk, named Franki, had been killed. Blood stained the back wall from the head shot.

"What else do we know about these guys?" the eager officer asked.

"They're sloppy," Van Buren said, nodding toward the bloodstain on the wall. That is not exactly true, he thought. So far they had done a fairly good job of covering their tracks, leaving only the dead bodies and very little evidence in their wake. The CSI's last report on the jewelry heist indicated that there still wasn't enough to go on. Van Buren had already known that. He had handled all of the evidence himself and had come to the same conclusion.

Van Buren could hear the radio in his unmarked car crackle to life. The voice from dispatch carried over the gas station and into the now open-air mini-mart. *"Zebra Four, come in."*

Van Buren walked out of the building—right through the blasted-out window—and over to his car. He reached into the car and grabbed the mike. "Zebra Four. Go ahead."

"We just got a report of a multiple car accident and shots fired five miles south of your position," the dispatcher reported. *"The patrol car missing from your location was involved. Check and advise."*

"Zebra Four. I'm en route." He released the mike.

Van Buren paused for a moment to take in the situation one last time before moving on. The only thing he could think was that the cops somehow realized who the robbery crew was, and that led to the fireworks. It made no sense to him, though. The descriptions on the crew were vague. Three white men, one white woman, and a black man, was pretty much all they had to go on.

A crew that size and description traveling together in one car might have made the cops take notice, but they weren't going to go around arresting every group that matched that description. Considering what Van Buren knew about the criminals, he assumed that their Armani-wearing leader could talk them out of most situations. That meant something must have gone wrong with someone else on the crew.

Van Buren got into his car and hit the highway. There was a chance this could all end at the accident site. Logic would dictate that he should bring backup, but the last thing he wanted was to have a contingent of justifiably angry officers on scene, ready for a fight and looking to avenge the deaths of their comrades. No. He would go in and secure the area before calling anyone. Van Buren wanted to make sure this played out exactly as he intended it to.

The criminals had taken a hostage; the wife of that marine, John Triton. He must have given chase. Since Triton took the cruiser, Van Buren assumed that the kidnappers had taken Triton's vehicle first. So in addition to killing a cop and a clerk, and injuring another officer, the perps had involved two innocent civilians. The fact that one of those civilians was a Marine—who, by Officer Kelley's tone, Van Buren took to be someone that should never have gotten involved in this nightmare—made the situation even more dangerous.

Van Buren revised his estimate of the heist crew. They *were* sloppy . . . incredibly so.

A couple miles up the road from the gas station, he found evidence of where Triton must have caught up with the Navigator. Shattered glass littered the highway. Van Buren called in the location, but barely even slowed. Trouble could be going down at that very minute, and he needed to be involved in reining it in.

It wasn't hard to follow the path of the two vehicles. Debris and skid marks decorated the highway. A construction site seemed to bear most of the destruction. As Van Buren carefully made his way around the still stunned workers, he saw what appeared to be the top of the squad car lying upside down beside a two-ton scoop. He called in to report that location as well, without bothering to stop to speak with the witnesses.

Shortly past the construction site, Van Buren saw skid marks indicating that the chase was taken off-road. He followed along. Considering that his own car was not handling the shabby road conditions well, he could only imagine how the battered cruiser made its way through on the high-speed chase. All signs were pointing to the fact that this ex-Marine was not someone to be messed with. For Detective Van Buren, that could either be really good or really bad.

John Triton sat back in the trees and watched the flames continue to burn on the river's surface. His entire being was screaming for him to go after Kate. With every passing second, she was getting farther away from him. But he couldn't leave just yet. Someone was coming through the trees. At first, he thought it might be the kidnappers returning to the scene, but he quickly scratched that idea. Triton had checked out the Navigator and had seen that it was useless. It wasn't like there was any other reason for them to hang around. The kidnappers would have wanted to get as much distance from the crash site as possible.

That meant whoever was coming through the trees would probably be help. Either it was the police coming to check up on the accident reports, or it was someone else who had heard the commotion and was just coming to check things out. Triton didn't much care who it was. He just hoped that the person had a radio or a cell phone or something on them he could use to contact the authorities.

Triton needed to make sure that the police knew his wife had been taken hostage so she didn't get hurt in the crossfire when the murdering kidnappers were found. At least one of the cops had died back at the gas station. That meant the entire force would be out looking for the killers. Even though Triton would appreciate the help, he had every intention of handling this as he had each of his missions while in the Marines; as if he was the only one who could get the job done. Kate was too important for him to leave her rescue up to anyone else.

Once he filled the cops in on what happened, he would go after Kate. It was a big swamp, and he thought that she was probably going to be safe until her kidnappers got out of it successfully. Triton had no doubt that he could catch up with her.

The reality that he was just one man, and he had already been through a lot in the past hour, was also hitting. He needed a moment to catch his breath. But if the person skulking through the trees didn't show himself soon, Triton would be gone. He wasn't going to wait too long.

After another minute a man walked out of the brush, wearing an inexpensive suit and leading with his gun. It didn't take Triton's advanced surveillance training to realize that the guy was a detective.

Triton slipped out from the trees behind the man, still dripping swamp water. The man sensed a presence behind him and turned, holding his gun high. Triton knew he could easily disarm the man if it became necessary, but he hoped the detective would just hear him out and them let him go on his way.

"They've got my wife," Triton said by way of introduction.

"Detective Van Buren," the man said, holding up his badge. "SCPD. I'm going to assume you're John Triton."

"I didn't do anything," Triton said quickly, hoping to get that part out of the way. "They took my wife."

Van Buren seemed to be checking Triton out. He knew he was a sight, soaking wet and banged up, but he didn't care. He hoped the detective would take his appearance to show just how motivated Triton was in making sure these people paid for taking Kate.

"This is a matter for law enforcement now," the detective said. "Let us handle it."

"I've already seen them kill three people," Triton said, assuming the second cop back at the gas station didn't make it. "My wife will not be number four."

"I can't give you permission to pursue."

"I'm not asking for permission."

Triton glared at the detective. Had he waited for permission in Afghanistan, three Marines would be dead now. He was not about to let Kate die either. His mind was set. He was already wasting too much time. Triton wasn't waiting for the detective's blessing, but he didn't need the cops getting in his way either.

Van Buren slipped his walkie-talkie off his belt and spoke into it. "Zebra Four. I'm at the scene. Found both missing vehicles. One underwater."

"*Any sign of the suspects?*" the dispatcher asked in response.

Van Buren allowed the question to linger in the air a moment. He looked Triton straight in the eyes. Triton met his stare without blinking.

"No," Van Buren replied. "Nothing."

Triton was glad that the detective understood him.

Van Buren shut down his radio and hooked it back onto his belt.

"This area is tidal," Van Buren said, making a last attempt to dissuade Triton. "The way the water level changes, these guys are going to be impossible to track."

Triton didn't need any warnings. At this point they were just wasting time. "I grew up in this," he said, starting to walk away. "I can handle it."

"Triton," Van Buren called after him.

Triton turned to look back at the detective. His face has softened, looking more sincere, yet dead serious at the same time. "I've seen what these guys can do . . . you need to hurry."

It was advice Triton didn't need to hear, but he appreciated it all the same. He processed the information and continued into the swamp. As he moved along, he heard Van Buren behind him making contact with dispatch again.

"Get the chains out," the detective said. "I've changed my mind. I want this river dragged. We in the air yet?"

Triton was glad to hear that air support was in the mix. He did wonder why Van Buren was going to have the river dragged. If someone was in the water, Triton would have told him. They weren't going to get many clues from the remains of the cruiser either. The kidnappers had been in the Navigator.

Granted, it could have just been a cover to allow Triton time to get away. But he'd have preferred as many people as possible out looking for Kate instead of providing cover by needlessly dragging the river.

Triton made his way along the riverbank, silently and deliberately. He was in stealth mode, only stopping to listen for any sounds from Kate or her kidnappers.

His past training would kick in soon enough. Triton had learned a lot while training to become a Marine years ago. His recent experience in the desert would help greatly, but desert tracking and tracking through a swamp were two different things entirely.

Triton wasn't lying when he told the detective he had grown up in the swamps. At first they had been a playground for him, someplace he could sneak off to as a child. He didn't have many friends when he was young, and his father was away on business all the time. It was either stay at home for his mom's afternoon teas or go off exploring. The neighborhood had bored him by the time he reached ten, so he started venturing farther and farther until he found the exciting geography of the swamp. Sometimes he would spend the entire day exploring the marshy land. His mother never once asked him where he had been. Even when she was upset with him for tracking mud and muck into the house, she expressed very little interest in where the mud had come from. It was obvious, though, that he certainly hadn't gotten caked in it while playing on the family's beautifully manicured lawn.

By his teen years, Triton had turned his swamp ad-

189

ventures into a more serious way to pass the time. The land was perfect for long runs that would work every muscle in his body. He even brought Joe out a couple times. Playing football in the swamp prepared him for anything that he would meet on the field.

It was in the swamp that Triton had realized his future was to be a Marine. It had started innocently enough. While playing alone, he imagined himself a soldier in Vietnam. Before he even understood the meaning of war, he had reenacted many battles using the trees as his enemy and rocks as the prisoners he needed to free. It was often surprising to him how much those early games had helped him during his missions.

Now he was back in his element, but this time it wasn't a game.

His eyes continually swept the ground for clues. A freshly broken tree branch led him to a patch of trampled groundcover just ahead. Confident that he was on their trail, he proceeded with caution, knowing that he would find Kate soon and make everything right.

20

Kate slowly regained consciousness. She still wasn't quite lucid enough to know what was happening, but she was aware of images flashing through her mind. John was the first thing she saw. He was in his dress uniform. It was the day of their wedding. They both had wanted a small wedding: just them, her family, and a few friends at a little white chapel. She had never felt so much love as she did that day.

Then other images of John came to her mind. First were the ones she created on her own. The nightmares she'd had while he was on tour. The joy of seeing him that day he had come back to her for good. Had it only been two days ago?

She saw his stony face as the borrowed squad car slammed into the back of the SUV.

She saw the guns all taking aim at him.

She saw the explosion by the river as he left her once again.

She had to push those thoughts aside. There would be time to mourn later. First, she needed to escape.

Suddenly, Kate's mind was fully alert again. She kept her eyes closed for a moment, not wanting to let her captors know she was awake before she could assess the situation. Someone was carrying her. She wasn't sure how long she had been out, but they couldn't have gotten too far. It wouldn't be easy carrying someone through the swamp, no matter how muscular the person beneath her felt.

There was still a slight stinging where Angela had hit her. It was just enough to help marshal Kate's anger toward a useful purpose. She channeled her hatred into her resolve to escape. Her hands were still tied. That was a concern, but one she could work around.

Kate hadn't grown up looking for refuge in the swamps like John had, but she wasn't a stranger to the area either. Anyone who grew up in the county made it into the swamps at least a couple times as a child for one reason or another. This swamp was the site of her earlier fishing trips, before Mount Cedar. There was a good chance that if she got away from her kidnappers, she could find a place to hide out until someone located her.

The police were bound to find her eventually. The group hadn't exactly made a quiet escape from the gas station. Even if the police weren't looking specifically for her, Kate knew they'd be looking for her kidnappers. She wasn't sure what they had done to put them on the run in the first place, but blowing up a gas station and killing at least one policeman in the process would put them on the highest priority.

Kate opened her eyes, but only as little slits. She still didn't want to tip anyone off. Once she adjusted to the bright light slipping in, she noticed darker skin on the arm of the person holding her. It was Morgan. She rolled her head to the side as if it had fallen that way of its own accord. Bennett and Vescera were behind her. That meant Angela and Rome were in front.

Her best chance was with surprise. She knew she couldn't take them all, especially since they were armed. But if she could manage to get off Morgan's shoulder, she could go for the clump of trees and disappear. It was her most likely avenue of escape.

Kate waited. She tried to convince herself that she was still building her resolve, but deep down she knew that was a lie. She was afraid. It made perfect sense to her, seeing what this group was already capable of doing. Once she realized she was just stalling, she opened her eyes and started flailing on Morgan's shoulder. She lashed out at Vescera and Bennett, as they were nearest to her. She wasn't expecting to do any real damage, but hoping her wild actions would force Morgan to let her go.

It didn't take long. Morgan dropped her onto her feet. As soon as she hit the ground, she threw a vicious knee into Morgan's body. As she turned, Angela came up on her. Kate slammed her body into the woman, but Angela held her own.

The two women struggled. If Kate could get the upper hand, she could use Angela as a shield to get to safety. It would have been easier if Kate's hands weren't bound, though. Unfortunately, the fight didn't last long. Kate managed to throw Angela out of the way, but she soon felt the barrel of Rome's gun pressing into her head.

It wasn't the best plan, but Kate had to do what she could. John would have expected nothing less from her. And she wasn't going to let him down if he was watching over her.

Angela dusted herself off and sauntered back to Kate. "If we're gonna be friends," she said, "you'd better learn some manners."

Angela slapped Kate hard across the face. The impact stung, but Kate refused to cry out. She only glared at Angela, refusing to give the woman that satisfaction.

Rome wasn't about to say anything, but this woman was impressive. Kate had been through hell, lost her husband, and still managed to keep her fight. Other people would be whimpering in a corner over less.

Morgan, however, did not seem as impressed. He looked at Rome with disgust. "To hell with this!" he said.

Oddly, Vescera took that moment to sit down by a tree and take out his knife. He started playing with it, cleaning the dirt out from under his fingers, as Morgan came undone. Rome found it strange that Vescera of all people would choose to sit this one out, considering Morgan had been his suggestion in the first place.

Rome focused his attention back on Morgan. "You got a problem, brother?"

Morgan actually looked surprised by the question. "My *problem* is walkin' around a dirty-ass swamp with a man who has the entire county lookin' for him."

This was rich, since Morgan was the one who had taken things to the next level. The county was looking for him as much as any one of them.

"You killed those cops," Rome reminded him. "Both of them."

"Oh, so now we gonna start playin' the blame game," Morgan said, making no sense to Rome whatsoever. "Always gotta be the black man. Car gets stolen, black man did it. House gets robbed, black man. Cop car gets blown up by an Israeli, single-shot shoulder fired, rocket launcher, guess who?"

"The black man?" Vescera said, enjoying this far more than he should have been. Rome shot him a disgusted glare.

"That's right, Vescera," Morgan ranted on, drawing his gun, "very good. The black man."

As Morgan ended his tirade, his eyes fell on Rome, silently challenging the man. The two men locked stares for a moment as Rome tried to read the situation. Morgan was insane. That much was clear. And he was dangerous too. But the question was, was he dangerous to Rome?

In Morgan's eyes, Rome saw that the answer was negative—at least for the moment. Morgan reinforced this as he blinked first, backing down and allowing Rome to continue as alpha male.

But something had to be done. Things were getting out of hand.

"Vescera," Rome said, "why the hell would you bring this crazy son of a bitch into my crew? Besides, nobody's killing anyone until I give the go-ahead."

Without giving Vescera a second glance, Rome turned his gun and shot the man point-blank in the head. Any residual look of challenge was gone from Morgan as he stared in wide-eyed astonishment at Rome. Vescera's knife dropped onto the riverbank as his body slid down and disappeared into the water.

"What the hell was that?" escaped from Morgan's mouth.

"The go-ahead," Bennett answered wryly.

The crew watched Rome, stunned, as he holstered his gun. Even their hostage looked more terrified of him. And that was exactly what he had been going for. "Let's move out," he said, and started walking.

Rome didn't get far, though. Bennett grabbed his arm, but it was Angela who questioned him.

"What the hell was that?" she asked.

"You never know when you're gonna need a crazy son of a bitch," he replied simply as he removed his arm from Bennett's grasp.

He could tell by the look on Angela's face that she wasn't going to be a problem. She loved this side of Rome. Morgan was probably now realizing how close he had come to being the target, so he'd be okay, at least for the next couple hours. Bennett was the only concern, but he seemed to already be calculating his new share in the take now that Vescera was out of the mix.

Their attention was pulled offshore for a moment as a cluster of alligators rushed into the river and tore Vescera's body apart. Rome found it to be an interesting sight. To go from being alive to alligator food in mere moments was some kind of statement on life. He just didn't care enough to figure out what kind of statement it was.

"I thought you said there were no crocodiles," Morgan said to Bennett.

"Those are alligators," Bennett replied casually. "They're everywhere."

Van Buren sat behind the wheel of his unmarked car, slowly driving through the back roads of the swamp looking for anything out of the ordinary. Not that he would be able to entirely distinguish some of the things that would be out of place in a swamp. Traditionally, he spent most of his days and nights downtown.

From time to time a dead body was found dumped in the swamp, and he was called in to investigate. Even then his searches usually led him out of the swamp and back to civilization, where the suspects lived in nice little houses with white picket fences.

Outside of work, he wasn't big on spending his off time in the wetlands. Hunting and fishing weren't high on his list of pleasure-time activities. He preferred the finer things in life; a nice glass of Johnny

Walker Blue to accompany a good steak. Unfortunately, his insufficient paycheck did not suit that lifestyle at all.

Once again, Van Buren was glad that he had managed to take the lead in the investigation. He had waited back at the crash site only long enough for the team to arrive to begin examining the newest crime scene. He suspected that they weren't going to find too much that would be considered helpful, but he believed in leaving no stone unturned. His instructions were for a thorough investigation of the area while he went after the thieving, kidnapping cop killers. That was the only way to ensure the day played out according to what his plan.

As Van Buren looked through the trees, his radio came to life with the voice of Officer Kelley. The young buck was proving quite helpful in doing everything Van Buren told him to do, even down to the minutiae.

"What d'ya got?" Van Buren asked.

"Nothing yet," the officer replied. Van Buren could hear machinery working in the background, and guessed they were pulling the police car onto the shore. *"There's no way anybody could have lived through this."*

"Keep me informed," Van Buren replied, cutting off communication.

This John Triton was an impressive man. He hadn't needed to hear Kelley's comment to convince him of that. He just hoped that Triton would help him rather than hinder him. Van Buren had taken a risk when he'd allowed Triton to go after his wife. This could turn out any number of ways, but he was hoping that Triton would make his job easier instead of more difficult.

John Triton moved through the South Carolina swamp, watching and listening for any signs of Kate and her captors. He was lucky that they weren't well practiced at stealth. He had certainly tracked more difficult prey over the years. Even the rare times that the neighborhood kids had asked him to join in on their games of Capture the Flag had been more challenging than tracking this crew.

Footprints and broken shrubbery lined the path before him. The prints came and went in the soft mud. Some areas were just too wet to hold a good impression for long, but the overall trail wasn't hard to follow.

At first, Triton had been bothered by the fact that there was only one set of prints belonging to a woman. But he noticed that one of the men's prints sank deeper in the ground, and assumed that Kate was being carried. He didn't want to think about why she wasn't able to move freely on her own. On second thought, though, if she were dead, they wouldn't have bothered carrying her at all.

It was helpful that most people didn't normally stomp through the swamps on a typical weekday afternoon either. There were fewer tracks to follow and less signs to lead him astray. Triton wasn't worried that he was following the wrong trail. The grouping of four men and one woman was going to be easy to catch up with on his own.

As he walked, he came to a spot that was littered with signs that his quarry had recently been there. The kicked-up dirt and deep marks in the ground indicated that an altercation of some sort had taken place. By the depth of the footprints, it looked like most of the scuffle was between two women. Kate must have managed to get off her captor's shoulder and decided it was time for them to pay. He wasn't surprised to find that Kate was a fighter. She was a strong woman. He probably wouldn't have fallen in love with her in the first place if she weren't.

It was the blood on the ground that concerned him. The trail of blood leading to the water was not in the same place where the fight had happened, but it was bothersome, to say the least. A cowboy hat floated in the water, while some rather sated-looking alligators lined the bank across the river. There was blood in the water too. He hoped this only meant there were one or two less targets for him to neutralize. He didn't want to think about any other possibility.

The most interesting discovery along the riverbank was that of a hunting knife. Triton snatched it up and carried it with him as he continued along the route. He confirmed his suspicions in the mud when he saw the footprints continue.

Two women were moving along the trail now.

Maybe Kate's outburst had resulted in her getting more freedom of movement. More importantly, there were now only three men moving downriver. He wondered if Kate had managed to take one of her captors out, but figured that couldn't have been the case. He doubted that she would have been left alive if she'd killed one of the kidnappers. No matter how useful a hostage she might be to them, she wouldn't be left alive long enough to be a threat to the other criminals.

No, it was far more likely that the infighting had begun. Triton now doubted that the escapade at the gas station had been part of the original plan they had hatched. He didn't care about their motives, really. He just wanted his wife back. If they started killing each other off along the way, it just made Triton's job of saving her a bit easier.

The sound of a ringing cell phone cut into the silence of the swamp. Rome was amazed that he got reception out here. The plan he had signed up for had definitely been worth it. Morgan and Bennett looked dubiously at their leader as Rome checked the screen.

He had been expecting this call sooner or later.

"Hello?" he replied as he put the phone to his ear. "How you doin'?"

His silent partner was on the other end, totally missing the whole "silent" part altogether. He was screaming his head off. Even though they had a surprisingly clear connection, his words were barely intelligible.

Rome cut him off. " Oh, not so good, huh? Well, real quick, you know that double homicide I was just in?"

"You mean the dustup at the gas station?" his partner asked over the phone.

"Yeah, that's the one."

"I may have heard something about it," the worried voice said. *"You guys aren't exactly moving under the radar!"*

"I know. *Bad*," Rome said, indicating that he really didn't care. "Anyway, I think I've added kidnapping to my litany of atrocities. Actually, I'm sure of it, because she's standing right in front of me right now."

A blast of anger came through the phone that didn't even resemble words.

Kate shot him an evil glare, too. Rome was resigned to the fact that he wasn't winning any new friends today. Actually, just as he felt about the additional crimes of the past few hours—he didn't much care at all.

"So why am I telling you all this?" Rome asked, rhetorically. "Well, in the middle of blowing up a gas station, killing a Marine, and kidnapping, I came up with a great idea! I even came up with a great name for it! It's called *You're Out!*"

Rome laughed at his own genius. He was making up his new plan as he went along. It had come to him the moment he heard that blowhard on the other end of the line. *How dare that jackass talk to me like that?* Rome was the one doing all the heavy lifting in this operation.

It was then that Rome realized he could find some-one else to fence the diamonds for him. It wasn't like it would even be difficult. They weren't talking about unique artwork. Once he got out of the state and there was less heat on, he'd be able to find a guy to make the deal. He would probably even split the diamonds up between fences to make the stones harder to track. He knew about these options when he accepted the job, but everything had fallen into his lap earlier, and he figured, why should he bother doing more work than necessary? Now he was ready to cut people out; the job had turned out to be more costly than he had intended.

"Which basically means," Rome continued to clar-ify his new brainstorm, "you're getting nothing. No split, no payoff, no diamonds. No nothing," he paused. "I know we had a plan, but now that plan's changed. Well, for one of us. You see, I hold all the cards, and if you think for a second that you're gonna be able to—"

There was a clicking on the line. Call waiting. Rome checked the screen on the phone. At first he didn't recognize the number, but then he realized who it was—yet another call he had been waiting to re-ceive. Once again, he silently praised his cell plan.

"Hold on a second," he said, then clicked over. "Hello?"

As the person on the other end spoke, Rome saw that his crew looked content with his new plan. He fig-ured now they all were calculating their new windfall in having another partner out of the equation. Well, maybe not Morgan. He seemed to be in on the job purely for the fun of blowing things up. But after Chris, Vescera, and the guy waiting on hold, they were also probably wondering which one of them would be next on the hit list.

"Uh-huh, that's right," he said to the new caller. "Now, that includes all the premium channels and the sports package. Great. When will that be installed? See you then. Thanks." He clicked back to the other line. "Hello." No one was there. "Hello?"

How rude.

Rome shut his phone as he heard a familiar noise off in the distance. It figured that he'd be hearing it soon enough. Actually, he had expected it a bit earlier.

Everyone else froze at the sound, as if they were surprised by it.

Kate, however, did not even bother to contain her excitement.

"Helicopters," Rome said, acknowledging the sound of the choppers approaching. "Nice."

21

The sound of the helicopter sent a thrill through Kate. Even with Rome and his crew pulling her into the trees, it made her rescue much more likely. If the police had people in the air, they must have people on the water and on foot too. It was only a matter of time.

Rome had mentioned something about diamonds earlier. She assumed they were wanted for some kind of robbery. That, combined with killing a police officer and blowing up a gas station, meant that *many* people were looking for this bunch of lowlifes. That fact alone made her position considerably better. They were going to need to keep her alive for bargaining power at some point. Even though they hadn't really shown a predisposition toward much logical thought before, her odds of survival seemed to be increasing.

As the helicopter approached, Kate considered making a run for it. It was only a few feet to the tree line. If she moved quickly, she could probably get enough distance to keep the trees between her and their guns. All she needed to do was reach the clearing. Never before had a few feet seemed so close and so far away at the same time.

"You want to scream, don't you, Kate?" Angela asked. "Go ahead."

Obviously Kate had waited too long for the moment to pass. She briefly considered taking Angela up on the offer, if only as an act of rebellion. She knew it was pointless to yell from the trees. The pilot would never hear her over the helicopter blades. Then again, there could be people in the swamp around her at that very moment.

Kate lifted her chin slightly, and Angela responded by pressing her knife up against Kate's throat.

"C'mon, baby," Angela whispered. "Do it."

Kate froze. The knife was pushing into her skin. It would only take one flick of Angela's wrist to end her life. The woman's face was only inches away from hers. Their eyes were locked in defiance.

As the helicopter flew past, Kate backed down. There would be time for a move later. At that very moment, Kate was working on another plan.

Angela hadn't managed to tie Kate's hands very well earlier. There was a slight amount of slack in the ropes. Kate was silently working at the knot behind her back, trying to look nonchalant.

She was actually kind of proud of herself for holding up so well. Rome shooting Vescera in front of her had hardly fazed her. She was around death every day at work, though it did look different under the controlled chaos of the hospital. This was the first time she had actually felt joy over someone's death, though. That bothered her a bit, but not very much, considering what these people had been responsible for.

The crew sat in the quiet of the swamp for a full minute after the helicopter passed. Sitting in silence bothered Kate more than hiking through the swamp. Here all she could do was think. While she tried to concentrate on ways of escape, thoughts of John kept coming back into her head. The police would have been called to the scene of the accident. They might have recovered his body already.

Kate stopped herself before she could start crying. Tears would just get in the way at the moment. Besides, she didn't want to give these people any sign or reason to think that they may have beaten her.

"Looks like the air show's over," Rome said, motioning toward the crew to continue. "Let's move."

The group walked along. Kate was sorry to see that they were staying in the trees. There was a much better chance of being seen if they walked along the river's edge. Although they were following the river, the group was smart enough to keep it in sight from a distance. Less of a chance of being seen from boats. Kate figured those would be next.

As they started up again, Rome took the lead with Morgan in the rear. Angela and her knife were on Kate's right, while Bennett had taken point on the opposite side. Even though they had managed to surround her, Kate's only concern was keeping Morgan from seeing that she was working the ropes behind her back. Luckily, he seemed to be too preoccupied with the swampland around them to notice her.

The hike through the swampy terrain was rough, but Kate was holding her own. She was much more comfortable in these surroundings than Angela seemed to be, not that the woman was complaining. There was just something about the way she was walking through the underbrush that seemed wrong. It could have something to do with her shoes. Obviously Angela hadn't dressed with the intention of mucking through the swamp. Kate was glad that her vacation plans with her husband had called for more sensible footwear.

At the thought of her vacation, Kate's mind once again went back to John. It was killing her to do it, but she had to push him aside again. It was the only way she was going to get out of this alive.

Kate refocused on the group, looking for weaknesses. If Angela was uncomfortable, Morgan was downright irritated. He kept swatting at mosquitoes and gnats, trying to make some headway at clearing them from swarming around him. He did seem to be overreacting to the few insects in the vicinity. Kate hardly noticed the bugs at all as she worked at her ropes. She couldn't swat them out of the way if they were bothering her any way.

She noticed that Bennett had stopped in his tracks. She followed his gaze to see a large snake slithering on a log to his right. She was surprised that it was the first snake they had seen so far on their trek. The swamp was just teeming with them. She knew most of the snakes weren't deadly, but she wasn't about to let anyone else share her knowledge. It seemed to her that it could have been the first real snake Bennett had ever seen in his life. She thought that it would be better for her if he was afraid of it.

All four of her captors were transfixed by the snake. Kate had seen bigger. She had been taking an environmental studies course as part of her biology requirement for school. There had been much more dangerous creatures during the class excursions through parts of this very swamp. Unfortunately, it was a big swamp, and Kate knew they were nowhere near the populated, "tour-friendly" sections.

Angela took hold of Kate's arm as she hurried the hostage past the snake. Rome, on the other hand, seemed to slow his step to the point where the women actually passed him. He was transfixed by the snake, but not as much as Morgan.

"That's a creepy-ass snake," Morgan said. "Slimy . . . scaly. It's terrifying. All these animals and bugs . . . I hate this, man. I ain't built for this stuff." He seemed to be taking this trek through the swamp way more seriously than a guy of his bulk should have been, as far as Kate was concerned.

"Think about it," Morgan continued. "How many brothers you see in *Deliverance?*"

"How many brothers even saw *Deliverance?*" Bennett mumbled, not seeming to really care for the conversation.

"Well, this one did," Morgan said. "And the answer is zero. Why? 'Cause brothers don't go camping."

"Why does it always have to be racial with you, Morgan?" Rome asked lightly. "Why do you feel the need to confine us all to labels? Can't we just be people?"

Rome stepped up to Kate and threw his arm around her. She liked it about as much as she liked the sociological discussion he was trying to pursue. Kate turned to face him, tearing holes into the man with her eyes.

"What do you think, darling?" Rome asked. "Am I right?"

She didn't even stop to think about her answer. "I think you are a psychotic bastard, and if John were here, you'd be dead."

"Okay," Rome said, considering her answer in a damningly amused and condescending way. "But John's not here, honey. C'mon, you remember that big boom? That was him. That was your husband."

Rome concluded his sick banter by holding his gun to her head. She stared into his eyes, almost daring him to pull the trigger. Her life had been threatened so many times over the past few hours that it was beginning to lose all meaning. Without John, she wasn't feeling like there was much to live for at the moment anyway.

Her refusal to back down was rewarded by a disgusting smile on Rome's face. He was actually enjoying himself. She could tell that the whole afternoon was nothing more to him than a source of amusement.

Rome lowered the gun and gave her a pat on the shoulder.

"Good talk," he said. He then used the gun to gesture toward the path. "Now, let's go, people."

Triton heard the helicopter approaching before he saw it coming toward him. He had plenty of time to take cover in the trees. Getting spotted would only cause problems. The search would be redirected to his area. Aside from taking the attention away from the true criminals, it would also manage to slow Triton. He hadn't seen any searchers yet, other than the chopper. He figured that Van Buren would have pointed the search in the direction he, Triton, had traveled, but he couldn't be sure. They may have been going out in all directions. Again, this was both good and bad for him.

The small helicopter continued on its way. Triton considered it a fairly useless means of searching. If this were the desert, it would be one thing. Considering the trees and the overgrowth, helicopters were ineffective for searching in the swamp, even when looking for people who wanted to be found.

The appearance of the helicopter bothered him for another reason as well. If Kate saw it as a means of escape, she might make a dash for a clearing to draw the searchers' attention. The problem with that would be that her captors would kill her before the chopper could even find a good place to land. It wasn't a serious concern, though; Triton knew his wife was smarter than that.

Triton continued to follow the trail along the river. Kate's kidnappers were smart enough to stay in the trees, but they were so stupid that they did not to hide their trail. They probably assumed that Triton was dead, but that didn't mean that the cops wouldn't be following them. They thought the police were just too far behind to catch up. Either that, or they just didn't know any better. The way the group was dressed, Triton figured it was the latter. They seemed the type of criminals better suited to office buildings, not backwaters.

It would have helped if Triton knew what they were running from that had made them so willing to kill a few cops and destroy the gas station. If he knew their crime, he'd have a better understanding of their goal. They had been heading south out of the gas station, so it made sense that they would be continuing in that direction. Eventually they'd head to the marina. Triton knew there were some buildings along the river before that, though. It was possible that they might find a safe place to stop or someone who could help them escape before long. He stepped up his hike.

As he walked, Triton saw an old familiar tree, split in half down the middle. He knew exactly where he was. That tree had fallen on the worst night of his life—the night that he knew he no longer had a family.

After his "conversation" with his father about joining the Marines, John had gone for a walk to clear his head. Though some would call it a long-distance hike, it was nothing more than an evening constitutional as far as John had been concerned at the time. He knew that heading into the swamp as a storm approached was foolish, but he didn't care that night. He was feeling reckless; more reckless than usual.

His mind was full of anger over his father's attitude and the man's total lack of emotion. With each step, John's inner rage grew. By the time he reached a clearing in the swamp, he needed to let it out. As the wind whipped up around him and he was pelted by rain, he let out an earth-shattering scream. He continued to yell, not caring that he was being drowned out by the thunder. He had done this many times before when his rage took over. It was the only outlet that he felt he had. But this time it was different. This time he couldn't stop.

John kept screaming and yelling as the storm intensified. He was shivering and wet, but none of that mattered. He needed to release his anger. His throat began to burn until the storm sensed that he was through. A bolt of lighting shot from the sky, splitting the tree beside him in half. If it had hit another few feet to the right, he would have been fried. But John hardly blinked as he listened to the storm and began his slow walk home, knowing that from then on he would be a stranger there.

Triton shook himself out of the memory. He did notice the winds were starting to kick up, just as they had on that long-ago night. He didn't have time for

213

this. *Kate* didn't have time for it, either. With a renewed sense of purpose, he continued on through the trees, never once looking back.

A few minutes later, he came to a spot that his prey had clearly used as a rest point. Maybe they stayed there to wait out the helicopter as it passed overhead. If that was the case, then Triton was right on their heels. It wouldn't be long now before he had Kate back in his arms.

With renewed vigor, Triton ran flat-out through the swamp with the knife held tightly in his fist. The heavy vegetation was slowing his progress, but he knew that he was still moving faster than the group he was tracking. He figured that Kate had to be doing everything in her power to slow them even more. Choppers continued to circle the area overhead in a sweeping search grid.

Ignoring the air support, Triton slowed to search the ground for more recent signs of disturbance. The footprints here didn't match the ones he had been following. His prey must have veered off. He wasn't worried. The tracks had taken him this far. He could pick them up again.

Triton started to move off, but hesitated. There was something about the landscape that unnerved him. His combat instincts had taken over.

Knowing that it was dangerous to stay in one place too long, he carefully moved to his left. With his senses on alert, he felt the trouble before he heard the sound of the snap. His right foot broke a tripwire hidden in the underbrush.

A huge camouflage net suddenly sprung up around Triton. His feet were pulled off the ground as the netting violently hoisted him into the air.

As he flew up into the trees, Triton whipped the knife over his head, severing the net lines. As the netting continued into the air, he dropped fifteen feet down to the swamp floor. He landed in a fighting crouch, prepared for attack.

A huge redneck in stained overalls rose from the underbrush with a pump-action shotgun trained on Triton. It wasn't one of the kidnappers, that much Triton could tell. Of course, that didn't make him any less dangerous. The guy wasn't exactly holding a squirt gun.

"Hold it right there, cop," the man said.

"I'm not a cop," Triton answered.

"Don't lie to me, cop." The assailant threatened Triton with his gun again.

"I'm *not* a cop," Triton insisted again, moving to a slightly better position to attack.

"Don't move, boy."

The man pushed at Triton, who gracefully avoided the assault. Within seconds, the former Marine had the redneck's arm gripped tightly and his knife poised at his throat.

Triton was snatching the shotgun away from the man, grabbing the weapon by the barrel, before his enemy had a chance to recover. "I'm not a cop," Triton said, standing over the man. "I'm looking for some people—"

Triton never had a chance to finish his sentence. Something hard—it felt like a two-by-four—slammed into the back of his head. Triton briefly cursed himself for being caught off guard. Then everything went black.

22

A punch to the face roused Triton from his unconscious state.

Triton slowly woke up for what felt like the millionth time today. Before he could even open his eyes, he knew that he was not in good shape. Old leather belt straps bound him to what felt like an aged wooden chair.

As his eyes came into focus, he saw that he was inside an ancient wood-and-sheet-metal shack. Weeds were poking in through the rotting wood floor. The place looked like it could crumple from a light wind.

A table sat in front of Triton. It was covered with bottles, jars, and what looked to be vials of ether. His knife was jammed into the wood at the table's far end. This wasn't just some good ol' boys living in the swamp. Triton had stumbled into some kind of illegal activity. Again.

As if he needed formal confirmation on what he had come across, Triton saw brick-sized packages wrapped in foil stacked up along the walls. Drug-making paraphernalia lined the shelves and another table as well.

As before, Triton sensed the presence beside him

before he saw the man. A huge shadow loomed close by. The guy that had confused Triton for a cop earlier prodded him in the cheek with the business end of his hunting rifle.

"Easy, cop," the man said through a cheek full of chaw. "You ain't going nowhere."

His buddy crossed between the tables carrying armloads of the tinfoil bricks. He had probably been the one to knock Triton out. *A wimp-ass move, knocking a guy out from behind and not taking him on face-to-face.*

"How many other cops out there?" asked his interrogator.

"You guys got it all wrong," Triton tried to explain. "I'm not a cop."

The man backhanded him. Hard.

"Save your lies, boy," the man said.

"Cut off his fingers, Billy," the big thug said with a note of glee in his voice. "Then he'll talk."

Triton figured that they probably didn't get many visitors out here. These losers were probably itching for some action. It was really brave of them to attack a man strapped to a chair.

Triton ignored the thug and focused on the guy who seemed to be in charge.

Triton looked Billy in the eyes. He didn't expect that reason would work on the man, but he had to try something. "Listen," Triton said, "if I was a cop, I'd have a badge and a gun. I don't. I'm just trying to—"

Billy hit Triton again. Harder than the last time.

Triton gritted his teeth through the pain. He slowly turned back to face Billy with calm hatred in his eyes.

"I got choppers buzzing around here while you're sneakin' up our asses," Billy whined at Triton. "And you ain't no cop?" He snorted derisively.

Triton was done trying to explain the truth to this asshole. "Right . . . you're right," he said, formulating his plan. "I am a cop. They're tracking my GPS right now."

"GPS?" Billy asked, turning to the other guy. "I told you to search him."

Jeff's eyes about bugged out of his head. "I did!" he yelled back, obviously in fear of making Billy mad.

Billy looked at his captive. The criminal was angry before, but now he was seething. "Where's the god-damn bug, cop?"

Triton said nothing.

Billy turned back to Jeff. "Find it!"

Jeff didn't look happy, but he wasn't so dumb that he was going to go up against the guy with the big gun. He moved toward Triton, then thought better of that line of approach. Stepping around the chair, Jeff started searching Triton from behind, pulling at the collar of Triton's T-shirt as if he was really expecting to find something in the thin material.

Triton leaned forward, not wanting to make it any easier.

"Sit still," Jeff said.

Like there's a chance in hell of that happening, Triton thought.

Triton had timed his plan well. The noise had been off in the distance when he mentioned the GPS, but he was familiar enough with the sound to calculate speed and direction. The chopper was on its way.

Triton pulled away from Jeff again, moving himself into position and forcing Jeff to lean in farther.

As Jeff continued to pull at the back of Triton's neck, the police chopper skimmed the trees outside the building. The noise drew Jeff's attention, giving Triton his opening. In the time it took him to react to the noise outside the shack, Triton made his move. He slammed his head backward with the force of a pile driver, smashing into the other man's stomach.

The intensity of the blow made Triton's attacker double over. The former Marine repeated his back head-butt, connecting with Jeff's skull, sending the man stumbling backward. He collapsed, unconscious.

Triton quickly rose, pulling up the wooden chair by the straps. Before the other man could react, he smashed the chair against the ground, sending the old wood splintering.

Billy moved toward him, but Triton was not slowed. Both his arms were still strapped to the two halves of the chair, and he used them as weapons. Swinging his arms, he brought the remains of the chair back together around Billy's head. Wood fragments exploded in front of Triton.

Billy managed to keep on his feet, fighting back. He was clearly dazed, and stumbling slightly. Triton used that to his advantage, sending a flying kick at him that knocked Billy to the ground like a ton of tinfoil-wrapped bricks.

After a momentary pause from apparent shock, Billy managed to rally. He picked up a hatchet, took quick aim, and threw it at Triton's head. Triton quickly dodged the blade. He felt the wind from the flying ax blow past his head, then heard the thud as it embedded itself into a barrel behind him.

The two combatants rose, beating the hell out of each other in equal measure. Billy tried to connect with a left hook, but Triton ducked it, coming up with a jackhammer back fist.

Billy took the blow and grabbed Triton in a reverse bear hug. Triton managed to fight it off, connecting with a few fast elbows. The two of them smashed right through the other table, sending the rest of the contents flying about the room.

Triton didn't let the shooting pain in his back stop him. He was up on his feet in an instant, with adrenaline pumping. Billy was just as ready to continue the fight as he popped up as well.

Billy swung his left arm. Triton dodged the fist, and slammed Billy with a barrage of rib-shattering body blows. He followed the four blistering strikes with a series of breaking right-left-right jabs.

Rearing back, Triton charged Billy, ramming into the man with the force of a rhino. Triton slammed him into a concrete pillar. Triton deftly rolled back over the table, toppling a shelf of supplies over Billy for good measure.

Billy was done.

Triton stood amid the aftermath. The two men were splayed about the room, unconscious. The interior of the drug shack was totally wrecked.

Triton turned, snatched the knife off the table, and continued on his search for his wife.

23

It seemed to Rome that he and his crew had been walking for hours already. Rome checked the watch he had left the jewelry store with. Talk about taking a licking and keeping on ticking. It was odd that it would work so well, considering that the type of people that could actually afford watches like it hardly did anything that required them to break a sweat, much less own such a resilient piece of jewelry. Just one more folly of the rich that he soon intended to appreciate himself with his own newly bloated bank account.

The piece of beauty on his wrist indicated that it was getting near evening. The lengthening shadows in the swampland supported that. They had long since blown their meeting time. Of course, missing the appointed hour didn't matter now that Rome had canceled the meet. He wondered how his silent former partner was dealing with his exclusion at the moment.

A storm was brewing in the distance, both figuratively and literally. It was quite a way off, but he figured it was time to stop, take stock, and have a rest for a moment. Conveniently, he had found just the place to do that.

The river widened up ahead, becoming a sprawling wetland lake amid the trees. Set back into the still water was a large two-story fishing lodge. Rome didn't know much about the swamp, but he knew enough to know it wasn't fishing season. And even if he didn't know that, it was obvious that the lodge was empty. It had an abandoned look about it, even at this distance. It didn't seem the kind of place he'd like to hang, even if it was in season.

But more important than finding a place to rest was finding a potential means of escape. Just above the waterline of the lodge, Rome saw a dock with a boat tied up to it. He wouldn't exactly call the thing a yacht, but it was floating, so he knew it was river-worthy.

The sound of a motor was approaching from what he believed was the north, forcing Rome to pull everyone back into the trees again. The police were coming out in force using helicopters, boats, and whatever other means they could to get through the swamp. This boat held three cops: one at the wheel and two onboard. Rome watched as they docked the boat and the two passengers got off to search the building. That the officers were investigating there worked even better for Rome's planned rest. Once the building was cleared, there'd be no need to search it again for at least a few hours.

While they waited, Rome took stock of the lodge. An old Sinclair gas bubble fuel pump attached to an octane tank sat at the end of the dock for refueling.

That was good. Even if the abandoned boat was out of gas, they could probably fill it up.

The building itself was up on stilts, keeping it high above the water and the lower dock. That made sense. When a hurricane came through, Rome assumed the water level rose considerably.

Oil drums filled with what looked to be beer empties, machine parts, and hunting and fishing gear lined the rest of the deck running around the lodge's upper platform. Things were really going well for them finally. Now they had potential supplies.

Rome and his crew watched as the two cops cautiously entered the dark building. Their flashlight beams sliced through the lodge as they fought off the setting sun. One of the cops had gone down under the building, while the other took the main level. It seemed pretty dumb to Rome for them to split up like that, knowing they were after about a half-dozen criminals, but it wasn't really his place to criticize. His own people had been known to do some stupid things over the course of the past day and a half as well.

A glance to the side confirmed what Rome had already known. Angela had the foresight to press her knife up against Kate's throat again. Their hostage wouldn't be making any noise anytime soon. This was the closest chance she'd had to being rescued all day. Yet with the knife to her, all Kate could do was sit back, resigned, in desolate silence.

"We wait till they're gone," Rome whispered to his crew. "Then we go in."

The two cops came out of the building and mo-tioned to the third. As they went to board the boat, the "captain" picked up the mike to the boat's radio. It was so quiet on the water that Rome could hear both ends of the conversation.

"There's nothing here," the riverboat cop reported in. "We're headed for the marina."

"Search every shack from there to the marina," the voice on the other end ordered. *"Find them."*

Rome let out a smile. He had learned so much from that response. They might actually get away with this on several fronts.

Morgan started to move as soon as the cops floated off, but Rome grabbed his arm.

"What now?" Morgan asked.

"Now," Rome replied, "we wait. Make sure they're really gone."

"Man, you heard the guy on the radio," Morgan replied. "They're gonna be searching every outhouse down the river. They aren't coming back."

"We wait," Rome insisted.

And they did wait. Angela kept her knife on Kate the whole time. It worried Rome that their hostage wasn't saying anything at all. He didn't like her having all that quiet time to think of ways to make his day more complicated. After her previous outbursts, he wondered if she had anything planned. So after about five minutes, he motioned for everyone to move.

"All right," he said. "We go in . . . Maybe get some rest or a shower or—"

"Soup?" Morgan asked, sounding like a hungry child.

"Soup?" Bennett repeated with a scoff.

"Yeah. Warm, tasty . . ." Morgan was beginning to make even Rome hungry with his talk of food. Rome thought that it made sense that Morgan was hungry, since all he had for lunch was coffee. And Bennett never *did* grab the food he was supposed to be buying at the gas station mini-mart

"It's delicious," Morgan added about the soup.

"Okay, then," Rome said. He just couldn't help being entertained by the guy. "We'll go in and get some soup."

"Now that's what I'm talking about," Morgan said, still smiling like a child.

Rome had really warmed up to the idea of hiding out in the cabin. Aside from the possibility of getting some food, he realized he could tie Kate to a chair or something and not have to worry about her for a while. It would be nice to rest his mind as well as his feet for a moment.

The ground was particularly marshy on the walk to the dock. Rome had pretty much given up on his shoes. It was a shame, really. They were his favorite pair. Ultimately, he had decided it didn't matter. Once he got rid of the diamonds, he could get a whole new wardrobe to go along with his fancy watch.

In spite of the troubles they had and the unexpected encounters, Rome once again felt a bit of hope. With the police boat long gone, he suspected that the ground search was still focused back where they dropped off the Navigator. There was no way the foot patrol could have been moving as quickly as his crew was, since the police wouldn't have wanted to chance missing any clues along the way.

Bravado aside, for the first time since the gas station debacle, Rome thought that they were actually going to get away clean.

With that happy thought in mind, Rome led his crew over the creaking wooden pier to the lodge. Normally he wouldn't be caught dead in a place like this. But when the alternative was keeping to the swamp, where any number of trigger-happy good ol' boys were looking for him, he preferred this kind of joint to being caught and accidentally killed. Or killed on purpose, for that matter.

Morgan took the lead as they walked up the rickety old plank-steps to the screen door. Rome watched, perplexed, as Morgan carefully inspected the door frame. He shared a puzzled look with Bennett.

"What are you doing?" Rome asked Morgan.

"No contact points," he explained. "No alarm."

"Alarm?" Bennett asked. "What alarm? It's a *shack*."

Without further conversation, Bennett kicked the door open. The lock was so weak it busted right open, and the door nearly came off its hinges in the process. An ominous roll of thunder struck as they entered the dark lodge. Rome appreciated the sound effect for helping to set the mood.

The inside of the lodge had the look of a run-down

restaurant and bar. The bar sat at one end of the large room, along with some unstable-looking tables and chairs. An old hi-fi would serve as the jukebox when the place was open. LPs were stacked around it as if they had stepped through a time machine into the past. A Bose stereo system probably would have shorted out the entire electrical system in the ratty old building.

The place apparently doubled as a store for the hunters and fishermen in what had to be the oddest layout Rome had ever seen. Bait and tackle bins lined the side wall alongside a pair of coolers for beer, water, and soda. The electricity was obviously out in the whole place, because the coolers were dark too.

The place was decorated in Early Swampland. Nets, chains, rods, reels, and hunting gear were laid out on tables, waiting for hunting season to start. Rome thought some of it might come in handy should anyone sneak up on them unexpectedly. But the place was empty for the moment. Closed. Maybe for good. Certainly, for the better.

Rome took stock of the place with a disdainful eye. It was hot, humid, and smelled as if some of the hunters had left their prizes rotting on the premises.

"What died in here?" Bennett asked.

"I don't know," Morgan replied. "But it smells like baked ass."

Once again Rome silently questioned the level of class of the associates he chose to spend his time with of late. This was not exactly the kind of sparkling conversation he preferred to engage in with his contemporaries. It didn't matter, though. Pretty soon he'd be able to drop the losers and buy better friends.

He flicked a switch by the door, confirming what he already knew. There was no power to the lights, coolers, or fans. That would be the first order of business. He knew that the lights could attract unwanted attention, but if they were going to hunker down in there for a while, they'd need the place to be more comfortable than it was in its current state. Failing comfort, he'd settle for simply having the ability to breathe. The fans would help to get rid of the smell at the very least.

"Morgan, go see if you can find a generator," Rome said.

"Why me?"

"Why not?"

"Well," Morgan said, and Rome knew that whatever was about to follow was going to be good. Annoying, but good. "Maybe there's some guy out there with a hockey mask and a hatchet or a group of country-ass crackers craving some man-love."

Rome couldn't help but be amused by the guy. Morgan was unlike anyone he'd ever spent time with before, or hoped to ever spend time with again. But amusing him wasn't getting the job done, either.

"Hey, it'll be fun," Rome said. "Just like summer camp. Only different."

"C'mon, Rome, remember?" Bennett said jokingly

as he scoured the place for food and beer. "Brothers don't camp."

"Actually, I did camp once," Morgan said as his eyes glazed over in what Rome could only term a look of dubious reflection. "I was thirteen. I had this counselor, cool white guy . . . Timothy, Tim . . . or as he liked to be called, Johnny Whiplash."

Rome held back a laugh. He was curious where this was going. By the empty look on Morgan's face, he suspected it wasn't going to be a fun-time, happy camp memory. "Tell me, Morgan. What did Johnny Whiplash have to offer?"

"Well, first he offered me friendship," Morgan recalled. "Then some rock candy." His expression then began to change. His face was enveloped in fear, confusion, and sadness. "And then he offered me something I should never have accepted."

An odd silence fell over the lodge. It was clear no one really knew what to do with that information, or why the hell Morgan was sharing it in the first place. For the first time since they picked her up in the gas station, Rome shared a glance with Kate and knew they were thinking the same thing.

"Well . . . good luck with all that," Rome said, trying to break the tension. "Now, how about we go find that generator."

Morgan got up to make his way outside. He stopped before he went out the door, as if he had realized that he may have just crossed some sort of boundary with his true confession. "What we just talked about ain't gonna leave this room, right?"

"No, no, it won't leave this room, Morgan," Rome said, starting out calmly, but gearing up as he tried to control his anger. "But *you* will. Now go find the god-damn generator!"

Rome was beginning to grow tired of Morgan's antics. Blowing up cops was one thing, but dumping his repressed childhood crap on the crew was quite another. Rome was beginning to regret choosing to shoot Vescera. At least *he* knew when to shut up. While it was true that Mogan had some serious issues that needed to be addressed, Rome wasn't a freakin' therapist and wasn't interested in being the guy's personal counselor. He was beginning to think it might be better if they had one less person to split the money with.

Then again, if he wanted to get out of the swamp safely, Rome knew he had to put up with Morgan for a while longer. At the very least, he was someone to distract the alligators with, should it come to that.

"Hey," Bennett said as he went through the cabinets, "there *is* soup."

Morgan looked back into the room with an "I told you so" expression that was just so darn adorable that Rome considered letting the guy live a little longer. At least until they got out of the swamp.

24

Kate was beginning to worry that her kidnappers weren't just murderous, but certifiably insane as well. It certainly seemed that way with that Morgan guy. That just made it all the more important for her to get the hell out of there. On the bright side, she could feel that the ropes binding her hands had considerably more slack to them. It would only take a bit more work to free herself.

As she continued pulling at the knot, she took in the layout of the room. Angela was still nearby and probably wasn't going to leave her side without a good reason. Angela had taken Kate on as her own personal mission and was clearly taking that job seriously. Even if Kate went for the old tried-and-true "need to go to the bathroom" routine, she knew that Angela would come along. If she was lucky, that is. Rome seemed like the type of guy who was just as likely to send Morgan in with her.

Bennett was taking some canned food down from the cabinets. She thought that it might be possible to escape while they ate. All she had to do was clear the building and get into the trees. She was sure she could lose them with enough of a head start. It would be dark soon. That would help her get away, so long as she didn't manage to get herself hopelessly lost in the process. On the other hand, being lost for one night was better than getting killed by these trigger-happy lunatics.

Rome was busy studying a small pegboard that was covered with keys. Kate assumed one of them had to go with the boat docked outside. As Rome pulled a set off the board, she considered her options. If she could get those keys, the boat would provide a great escape—if she could manage to avoid being shot in the process. She could always grab the keys and hide out in the trees until she had an opportunity to take the boat. At least now she had some alternatives.

Content that she had the makings of a plan, Kate doubled her effort on the ropes. She was using the precision she had been training for in medical school to attack the knots with her surgeon's hands. Conveniently, Angela had sat her down on a stool with her back to the wall, so no one could see what she was up to.

Kate could feel the ropes finally loosen. One last loop, and she managed to free herself, catching the rope before it fell the floor. She looked around the room for her best escape route. She wasn't ready to make her move yet, but the time would come. Until then, she watched Rome, Angela, and Bennett warily.

Dark clouds were rolling in the sky, and distant thunder began to rumble. Triton ignored his ghosts from the past as he silently made his way toward the dock underneath the lodge. The man he'd heard the others call "Morgan" coaxed the generator to life in the cramped space beneath the building. Triton remained still as he waded in the water beside the dock. He needed the generator to be running first, to give him some time and a distraction. The group inside would be more likely to come out and investigate if it took too long for the lights to come on.

"There's your power," Morgan mumbled to himself.

Triton almost hadn't heard him. As the generator geared up, it started thumping and banging as he had suspected it would. There was no way an old rusted-out piece of equipment like that was going to function silently. In the lodge above him, Triton saw light coming through the cracks and heard music from a jukebox or something playing in the background. Between the generator noise and the music, he could not have asked for better cover.

Triton sank back into the water, moving to the side so that he had a better angle for his attack. He could barely see shapes above the murky water, but he suspected his movement had drawn the man's attention. The guy had come over to the edge of the dock. He was looking directly at Triton, but the murky water combined with the shadows would obstruct his view. Triton saw a large water turtle along the edge of the water, nibbling at some vegetation. Morgan saw it and shook his head as if that had explained any noise he may have heard.

Once Morgan turned away from the water, Triton decided it was time to make his move. He silently rose up and out of the water and pulled himself onto the deck, careful to make as little noise as possible. Gripping the knife he had taken from the dead man earlier, Triton quietly approached Morgan from behind. His strike was imminent when a squeak from one of the old boards could be heard over the thumping generator, giving away his position.

Morgan instinctively swung his arm back, slamming into Triton. The move caught Triton by surprise, causing him to drop his knife, which stuck in the dock. Morgan turned. There was a look of shock on his face, which made sense, considering he probably thought he was looking at a dead man.

Triton used that shock to his advantage, throwing a fist to the man's face. It connected with his chin. Morgan was thrown back, but recovered with his own punch that landed in Triton's gut. Triton's six-pack absorbed the blow as he went full tilt, throwing punch after punch at his opponent.

Morgan managed to block most of the punches, but the few that made it through did a fair amount of damage to the man's face. Morgan took a step back to regroup. Thinking that he had his opening, Triton went after the man. But this time, Morgan was prepared. He kicked his leg up and slammed it into Triton's chest, knocking him back several feet.

Triton was reeling from the blow, but the former Marine wasn't about to let it slow his attack. Morgan was about to go for the knife that was still stuck in the dock. Triton knew he couldn't—and wouldn't—let his enemy get it.

Triton took two steps before throwing himself into a forward roll and grabbing the knife. He completed his somersault, coming up with the weapon and thrusting the knife up into Morgan's chest. With an upward motion, the blade sliced through Morgan's body. Death was instantaneous. As soon as Triton released the knife, Morgan's body fell back onto the deck.

Triton stealthily slipped into the darkness beneath the lodge. Someone would be coming for Morgan soon, and he would be ready. He'd take them out one by one until Kate was the only person left in the lodge.

As Triton made his way to the edge of the space under the lodge, he heard footsteps above. Someone had come out onto the upper deck. From the sound of the footfalls, it had to be one of the men. Whoever was above him was twirling a set of keys. From the soft beeps Triton heard, it sounded like he was trying to make a call on a cell phone.

"It's Rome," the man said finally. "Plan A's screwed." There was a short pause. "We're switching to plan B. . . . No, I don't know what plan B is, I'm making this up as I go. . . . You know that place Rita's? Down by the marina? I want you to leave the car there for me. . . . No. As soon as you can. It looks like we're going to Phoenix."

Just what Triton needed, another bad guy to have to

deal with. He'd have to take everyone out now. No telling who else the guy Rome might have in reserve.

Triton ducked back down as Rome finished his call. On the bright side, he now had a backup plan in case he couldn't take everyone out at the lodge. He briefly considered just going to Rita's to wait them out. Maybe he'd have the time to get rid of whatever backup was waiting for them before they arrived.

Triton finally decided that he wasn't willing to risk Kate's life like that. Once they got to their getaway car, they probably wouldn't need her anymore. If Triton was going to save her, it would have to be now.

25

Kate's mind was working overtime on potential escape routes. Her hands were free, but she was still outnumbered four to one. She wanted to make her move before Morgan got back, but knew that it would be risky. It would also be pointless if she managed to get out the door or a window only to run smack into him.

Bennett was too close at the moment, anyway. He was fishing beers out of the cooler and lining them up on the bar. Kate doubted he would be offering her one, and honestly, a warm beer wasn't exactly what she was in the mood for anyway. She held her hands tightly together as he approached her, not wanting to give away the fact that she had gotten the ropes off her wrists.

"What are you looking at, princess?" Angela asked.

Kate just shook her head and looked away. Her plan was starting to fall into place. If she could manage to pit the group against each other, she might be able to find her window of opportunity. It wasn't like it was even going to be that difficult. Rome had already proven that he was ready to kill.

"Why so sad?" Angela moped falsely. "You don't like your new friends?"

Even though Kate knew she had no chance of winning the argument, she wasn't about to just sit quietly. She didn't care about getting through to Angela as much as she just wanted to get at the woman. "You're pathetic," she said, throwing as much condescending pity into her voice as she could manage.

"How so?" Angela asked, obviously happy that Kate had decided to play along. She was so smug, thinking that because Kate was supposedly tied up and sitting on the hardwood floor, she was going to roll over and play dead.

Kate motioned with her head to Rome, who was still out on the deck. "Him. You're like his little puppet." She laughed with pity. "It's pathetic."

It was clear she had struck Angela a good verbal blow. But the woman refused to go down that easily. "Actually, we're partners."

Kate was amazed by the weakness of the strong woman's defense. "Actually, you're deluded."

As Rome walked in from the deck, Kate could see that doubt and anger were starting to enter Angela's head. Kate had finally made a dent. Now she just needed to find a way to exploit it for her benefit.

"Bennett, you grew up on the water," Rome said, helping Kate's plan by ignoring Angela. "Louisiana, right?"

"Florida," Bennett corrected him.

"Whatever," Rome said ignoring the man's answer, as he tossed Bennett the keys from the pegboard. "Make sure that boat out there is good to go."

"On it," Bennett answered as he caught the keys and headed outside.

Kate thought that this might be her chance. If she could work her way past Rome and Angela and take Bennett by surprise on the boat, she might be able to get away. Either that, or she could head into the trees and wait. She just hoped she didn't run into Morgan on the way.

"Oh, yeah," Rome added as Bennett was almost out the door, "and while you're out there, Bennett, see if you can track down our little camper."

Bennett laughed as he continued out the door. Kate assumed that he'd do that part last. There was a good chance that she could manage to get out before either man came back. At least, that was her hope.

Triton slipped back under the building. He sensed that someone would be coming out to check on Morgan soon. He walked back along the deck, grabbed the dead man by his feet, and dragged him behind a pile of crates. The hiding place would do for now. Triton didn't expect that anyone would get this far. And if they did, they would have had to kill Triton to do it, so he really didn't need to worry too much about hiding Morgan's body any better.

A dull thud came from above. It was difficult to hear over the loud generator, but Triton thought it sounded very much like a body falling on the wood floor. Triton's concern for Kate increased. It could have simply been someone shutting a cooler, but he wasn't going to stop worrying until he saw once and for all that his wife was safe and sound.

He raised his body as far as he could, standing on tiptoe and straining to hear through the floor of the building. Triton was pretty sure he could make out three sets of footsteps above him. Kate must have been sitting. Maybe even tied to something. He refused to think there might be any other reason she wouldn't be moving with the other three.

One of the sets of footfalls seemed to be heading for the door. Triton quietly hurried along the deck, throwing himself behind a stack of oil drums. As the door above him opened, he caught the tail end of the conversation. It was difficult to hear over the noise of the generator, but Triton did his best to tune that out and focus. The guy named Bennett was coming out to check on the boat and look for Morgan. Knowing what he knew about this group already, Triton expected Bennett was going to go for the boat first. He slipped to the side of the oil drums so that he would stay in the clear when Bennett walked past.

Bennett exited the building above and climbed down the ladder to Triton's level. As expected, the man bypassed the area under the lodge and walked down the platform to the dock and the lone boat tied to it.

Triton silently made his way down one of the building's inner-leg struts. He moved stealthily around the platform behind Bennett. This time, he took extra care to keep his weight on multiple planks so the old wood didn't squeak beneath his feet and give away his position. He was helped by the fact that the generator seemed to be acting up more than it had earlier and was growing louder by the minute. He figured no one had actually tended to the machine, other than filling it with oil, for several fishing seasons. More than anything else, other people's simple laziness had helped him on many missions before. It looked like it would today as well.

Bennett moved toward the boat, examining it from all angles. He threw a set of keys up in the air and caught them. Triton could tell that this boat wasn't going anywhere anytime soon, no matter how many keys they tried. He doubted very much that a pretty boy like Bennett knew anything about boat repair. But even from behind, Triton could tell that the guy was ready to give it try. At least, he wasn't backing away and giving up altogether.

Triton moved closer to Bennett, moving painfully slowly and silently. His eyes were on his prey. Even though he made no sounds, he could tell Bennett's senses had gone on alert. Obviously the man had some training in his past. Bennett nearly caught Triton off guard as he spun around while grabbing for his semiautomatic.

But Triton was just a step faster. He counter-turned on Bennett and gave him a hammer punch directly to the right forearm nerve bundle. It was a well-practiced move he knew would force any opponent to drop his gun, as Bennett had just done. Triton was standing between Bennett and the lodge. The gun was nearly equidistant between them.

Without warning, Bennett erupted in an instant with a barrage of lighting-fast punches. From many years of practice, Triton was just as fast, if not faster. He managed to block or dodge most of the fierce blows, bobbing and weaving in a defensive stance. A few shots managed to break through and land. Triton wasn't surprised to find that there was power in the man's fists, but nothing that was too much of a concern to him. He stepped back for a moment to reassess his opponent. He wasn't about to underestimate the pretty boy again.

When Triton saw the opportunity, he struck with a monster blow to Bennett's chest. The punch knocked Bennett through the air, who landed on his ass several feet away and the wind knocked out of him. Again, he tried in vain to call out, but he was unable to scream. His lungs were empty.

As Bennett gasped for air, Triton calmly walked up to him, lifted his leg, and stomped on Bennett's neck. It would have been so much easier for Bennett if he had just turned Kate over to her husband. Since he knew that Bennett was only going to get in the way of her retrieval, Triton knew he had to take him out.

Once the cable was secured around Bennett's neck, Triton launched the man off the dock. The cord tightened with a satisfying crunch. Bennett's body continued to swing wide, and it was impaled on a piece of broken wood protruding from the underside of the lodge.

As Bennett was speared, Triton saw Detective Van Buren just past the now-dead body. The detective's gun was drawn. If Triton hadn't managed to take out Bennett, he knew Van Buren would have. Although he did wonder why the detective hadn't just made his presence known and arrested the man. Triton didn't regret killing one of the men who had taken his wife, but he preferred to save death as a last resort.

The detective lowered his weapon, and the two men regrouped under the lodge.

"How many are left?" Van Buren asked.

"Two," Triton replied with quiet anger. "And my wife."

"I'll call it in," the detective replied as he turned to leave.

Triton stopped him. "No time," he said. "Listen, the second they know we're here, Kate's in play. I gotta do this now."

"No," Van Buren said quickly.

Triton wouldn't hear it. He wasn't about to wait.

But apparently that wasn't what Van Buren had meant. "*We* gotta do this," the detective said. He nodded, indicating that they were in this together. Triton was glad to see that the detective understood him. For the first time in what seemed like forever, Triton finally had someone on his side aside from Kate.

"Do what you need to do," Van Buren said, "but remember, whatever happens here, you went in as my backup."

Triton nodded. He didn't give a damn about the paperwork afterward. He just cared about Kate. If Van Buren needed him to play the bureaucratic game to save his wife, then that's exactly what he would do. All that mattered was that he had gotten the go-ahead this time, unlike in his mission in Afghanistan.

Van Buren waved back to the loud generator. "You cut the power, and we go."

Triton nodded. He could hear footsteps directly overhead. Only two left to deal with, and he would have his wife. He took a deep breath to steel himself for what was about to happen. He wasn't worried about being ready physically as much as emotionally. No amount of training could prepare him for this kind of action. There had been plenty of times in the past when he had gone into a situation concerned about the welfare of hostages. But never before had he loved any of them.

"Ready?" Van Buren asked.

Triton crept over to the generator. It was banging and spitting so loudly now that they must have been hearing the noise inside the lodge. That worked to his advantage. If Rome and the woman with him thought the generator cut out on its own, Triton and Van Buren would maintain the element of surprise. So long as Rome didn't get suspicious that neither of his men had come back yet.

Triton pulled the control lever. With one last bang and a hiss, the machine was silenced, plunging the building into darkness.

26

"So, this whole thing," Kate said, continuing with her plan to bait Angela, "is about some diamonds?"

Angela couldn't manage to hide her surprise over hearing that Kate knew about their heist. "How did you—"

"I can hear, you know," Kate said. "His phone call back when we were still in the swamp. So, how much did you get?"

"That's really none of your business, missy," Rome said. She was amazed that the man could be so condescending and yet come across as a perfect gentleman at the same time.

"I'd say you made it my business when you kidnapped me and stole my car," Kate said. She wasn't able to say the other thing that they had done—taking John from her—out loud. "So all this over a few diamonds."

"A few?" Rome laughed as he reached into his jacket. For a moment Kate thought he was going for a gun, but he pulled out a velvet bag instead. "Take a gander."

Rome opened the pouch for her and held it beneath

her eyes. Kate was momentarily in awe. She had never seen so many diamonds before in her life.

"And here I was thinking that you guys were small-time hoods," Kate said. "Glad to know that the lives you've taken were all for the big bucks. That makes all the difference."

"Somehow, I feel that you're being sarcastic with me," Rome said as he closed the pouch and returned it to his jacket.

"I've got an idea," Kate said. "An offer, actually."

"I can't wait to hear this," Angela said.

"I'm not talking to you," Kate said. "The offer is for Rome. He's obviously the one making the decisions around here."

Angela looked like she was about ready to spit, but Rome held up a hand to calm her.

"Go ahead," Rome said.

"I don't know much about diamonds, but that sure looks like a lot of money you have in that pouch," Kate said. "When this is all over, instead of killing me, why don't you buy my silence?"

"Because it would be just as easy to kill you," Rome answered. "Easier, actually."

"Okay, true," Kate conceded. She never actually thought he would spare her life, but that wasn't the point. "But why be greedy? Technically you wouldn't even be losing any money. Just give me the share that would have gone to that guy you shot earlier. Or the guy you told over the phone was out of the deal. You've got plenty of extra shares around here."

"I still don't see what I'd get out of this arrangement," Rome said.

"Boy, you're kind of greedy, you know that?" Kate was actually enjoying herself. She liked the confused look on Angela's face most of all at the moment. "You're cutting people out left and right, and you can't even spare a few bucks for me."

"You'd seriously let us get away with it?" Rome asked, not seeming to believe her for a second. "After we killed your husband?"

Kate almost faltered, but she stayed strong. "It was worth a try. I mean, how many other people are you planning on cutting out of the deal? I figured there'd be more than enough money to go around come the end of the day."

A roll of thunder echoed through the building, as if to underscore Kate's words. She could see they were having an effect on Angela, at least. She seemed to be looking at Rome differently than she had been the rest of the day.

The conversation came to an end as lights began to flicker until they went out entirely, plunging the room into shadow. The thunderous hum of the generator beneath them subsided as it slowly powered down.

Kate hadn't expected the distraction, but she'd be a fool not to capitalize on it. Using her free hands, she pushed herself up off the floor and ran for the back door.

"Get her!" she heard Rome yell as she crossed the threshold without slowing down or looking back. She didn't have to check to know that Angela was already on her tail.

Kate jumped down the back stairs, not even touching one of the rotted old planks as she headed for the nearly empty parking lot. A road cut through the trees up ahead. If only she could make it into those trees, she could lose Angela and follow the road to safety. She couldn't be too far from a main thoroughfare. The lodge had to get its customers from somewhere.

Kate dove to the right, avoiding Angela's grasp as she continued her run for the tree line. She was only a few yards away when she felt Angela on her back. The bitch pushed Kate forward, forcing her onto the ground. But Kate was no victim. John had walked her through too many workouts in their makeshift gym garage. As soon as she hit the dirt, Kate grabbed hold of Angela's ankles and flipped the woman over her. Kate then jumped to her feet, giving Angela a good kick in the ribs.

"I owed you that," Kate said with an immense feeling of satisfaction.

Faster than Kate had thought possible, Angela managed to right herself and lunge. She grabbed Kate by the leg, tripping her up. In the time it took Kate to regain her balance, Angela was on her once again.

The two women came together, face to face, and locked arms. Kate's hands had balled up into fists. She felt the full force of the fury that had been building up inside her ever since John was murdered. She was yearning to release it.

"Go ahead," Angela said, tauntingly. "Try it."

And Kate did.

She unleashed her rage with a series of devastating blows against Angela's body. With each punch, she felt her anger intensify. She was unloading on Angela, finally giving the woman the ass-kicking she deserved.

Kate delivered blow after blow, sending Angela reeling. The woman was going down. Kate thought she had won, but at the last moment, Angela pulled her gun, forcing Kate to halt her attack. Kate froze, but it was clear to both of them who would have won that round, and Angela didn't like it.

"Playtime's over," Angela said. Getting in one last blow, Angela clocked Kate in the jaw.

Kate dropped to the ground, once again feeling the darkness envelope her. This time, she refused to go out. She wouldn't give Angela that satisfaction. She tried to hold onto her senses as best she could. Kate managed to remain conscious, but she couldn't stop Angela from tying her hands once again.

On the other side of the lodge, Triton charged toward the front door with Van Buren trailing. He knew that technically, the law officer should have taken the lead, but it was doubtful that Van Buren had half the training Triton possessed. The detective didn't seem to mind and was perfectly fine with standing back. As they reached the screen door, the detective gave a silent signal for Triton to go in first.

Triton burst through the door. The room was dark,

but there was still enough light to see by. In his haste, he had miscalculated, however. He failed to recon the area again before entering, and he was surprised to find that Kate wasn't in the room. As he turned back to check his support, he saw that Van Buren hadn't followed him in either. He was basically defenseless; a target bathed in the light from the doorway.

In the split second it took Triton to absorb this information, he saw that there was one person still in the room. It was the man who seemed to be in charge: Rome. He spun on Triton, in obvious shock over seeing the supposedly dead man. But he quickly managed to regain his composure.

"Now that's a crazy son of a bitch," Rome said as Triton glared at him from just inside the doorway. "I may not like you, but I do appreciate the balls. I gotta admit that."

Rome pulled his gun and fired. Triton dove for cover behind the bar as bullets tore into the glass bottles above his head.

"Let's hold the fire," came Van Buren's voice from the other side of the bar. This time he had decided to step in as opposed to just letting Triton do the dirty work for him.

Once the shooting stopped, Triton hazarded a look from behind the bar. The detective had used him to provide a distraction while he came in from behind to suprise Rome. Triton wasn't exactly thrilled with the plan. It had been a hell of a risk on his life.

Van Buren had the drop on Rome. The criminal

was forced to lower his gun. But something about the situation didn't read right to Triton. Van Buren seemed surprisingly nonchalant.

"No way," Rome said calmly, "you too? Wow, everyone's here. All we need is a clown. . . . We could have a party."

But Triton was in no mood for playful banter. "Where is she?" he demanded, coming out from behind the bar and moving straight for Rome.

Triton cleared the distance in a few leaping steps. He grabbed Rome by the collar, shaking him violently. The information the man possessed was the only thing keeping Triton from ripping him apart. Not that he wouldn't consider doing just that once he knew his wife was safe.

The detective, however, had other plans. Van Buren's gun was still up, but it was aimed at Triton now. Triton knew the detective had rules to play by, but he didn't care. If he had to beat the living crap out of the prisoner to get the information he needed, Triton was more than willing to do that. Besides, no one had read the man his rights yet. And since Triton was just an ordinary citizen, it didn't really matter how he got the information.

"Not so fast, big guy," Van Buren said, taking a step in his direction. "He's got something I need too."

At first Triton didn't understand what the detective was talking about. But then all the pieces started falling into place. Rome and his crew were on the run. Kate had been an innocent victim in their quest to get away from something. The detective was involved somehow. Maybe he'd been chasing these guys across the state. Maybe he had some kind of personal grudge.

This turn of events did not sit well with Triton at all.

The question of the moment was, what did Van Buren want? But that didn't really concern Triton at all. He hadn't asked to be part of this. He didn't want to be part of it either. Let Van Buren and Rome hash out their problems on their own time.

"Man, I only want my wife," Triton said to the cop as he let Rome go. "I don't care about you, and I certainly don't care about him. Just don't pull that trigger until I know where she is."

Triton took a couple steps away from Rome, trying to separate himself so Van Buren would have to focus on two targets instead of him and Rome locked together as one.

"Don't worry, Johnny," Rome said reassuringly. "He can't shoot me until he knows where the diamonds are. Because that's what he's after. Isn't that right, Officer?"

Triton looked to Van Buren. The detective didn't respond, but he didn't need to. The look on his face told Triton everything he needed to know.

"Why don't you take a second to let that sink in there, champ?" Rome said.

Triton was struck by the news that his hunch was right. His wife had been taken and his life thrown upside down over a robbery. People were dead, and he prayed that Kate wasn't among them. And the damn detective was in on it. Rome had gone and burned him. And Van Buren had let Triton track his partner down for him. Triton had taken out the rest of the crew while Van Buren sat back and let him do the heavy lifting.

A new kind of rage welled up inside Triton. It was unlike anything he had ever felt in war. Even Major Wilson bringing him up on charges could not prepare Triton for this kind of betrayal. The one person Triton believed was on his side—an officer of the law, no less—had teamed up with the bad guys. Triton could not abide that kind of dirty behavior. It put his anger on full boil.

The volcano was about to erupt.

27

Triton suddenly found a gun pointed in his direction. Triton wasn't sure when he had become Rome and Van Buren's mutual enemy. It seemed to him that they could let him leave with Kate and simply hash things out between themselves. Of course, now that Triton knew that the detective was involved, the odds of them being willing to leave him alive dropped considerably.

"That's far enough," Van Buren said. Triton had been attempting to shift his position so that he was more directly between the two men. If he could get them to turn on each other, he might be able to find a way out of this. But first he needed to understand what the hell was going on.

"What is this?" Triton asked, never wavering his gaze from Van Buren's gun. The detective was the immediate threat. Rome didn't have nearly as much to lose if Triton ID'd him. Hell, Triton wasn't even sure if Rome was really the guy's name.

"How'd you hook up with this Boy Scout?" Rome asked Van Buren.

"You really screwed this one up, Rome," Van Buren

said, forgoing the banter. "I handed you that heist. It was made. Quick in. Quick out."

Triton did not like how this was going. Van Buren had set the whole thing up. The fact that he was so willing to discuss his involvement this openly was not good. Triton suspected he only had a little time to get out of there before the detective started firing.

"It got crazy," Rome said nonchalantly. "I had to improvise."

Triton seethed that the man considered Kate as if she were some kind of "improvisation" on his plan. In that instant, he wanted to spring on Rome, to beat the man into submission. But he knew that's what Van Buren wanted him to do. Then the detective would just shoot Triton and take off with all the diamonds. Assuming Rome was dumb enough to have them on him at the moment.

"So did I," Van Buren said, shaking his gun at Triton. "You tried to cut me out. Lucky for me you picked the wrong hostage."

Triton glared at Van Buren. His anger was building. Now it was directed back at the detective. "You played me," he said through clenched teeth.

Hate trumped logic as Triton made a move for Van Buren. The detective wasn't having it, pointing his gun threateningly.

"You want a medal?" Van Buren asked.

"Now, I really don't want to alarm you or anything," Rome said to Triton, as if they were good buddies, "but I don't think he's gonna let you live. How can he? Seriously, you know he's a cop, and I went and let that little secret about the diamonds slip out,"—he looked to Van Buren—"Sorry about that."

The detective looked pissed at his partner. Triton didn't care about any of what was going on anymore. It wasn't like Rome was saying anything Triton hadn't already figured out. He was focused on finding a way out of this mess.

"Anyway," Rome continued, "it looks like you two have a lot of stuff to sort out, so maybe I should go."

Van Buren didn't agree with that part of Rome's plan. He directed his gun at the gang's leader. The detective only took his eyes off Triton for an instant, but that was all the former Marine needed. With blinding speed, Triton bolted at Van Buren, twisting toward the right and narrowly avoiding the shots from the detective's gun. Triton grabbed the man's wrists and held his arm at an angle that would make any additional shots useless.

Rome, however, was not hindered. He swung his gun at the two men and pulled the trigger.

Sensing movement, rather than seeing the gun, Triton swung himself around, keeping Van Buren in front of him. As Rome unloaded his weapon, Triton held up the detective as a human shield. Triton pushed the dying body forward on Rome as he dove for cover behind the bar once again.

He heard Van Buren's body drop to the floor. Dead.

Rome continued to fire into the corner where Triton had taken cover. Triton was pinned at the moment, but he was prepared to strike when he got the first opportunity.

Bullets continued to shatter the bottles above Triton as Rome fired blindly over the bar. As Triton considered his next move, he heard the brackets beneath the shelves on the wall above him start to give way. He barely had a moment to cover himself as the shelves collapsed, sending boxes, bottles, and fishing equipment down upon him. It was an odd assortment of debris, but that didn't matter. It was more than effective at temporarily trapping him behind the bar.

Triton was dazed, but not out. He heard scuffling sounds. Rome was probably searching Van Buren's body for his weapon. Then Triton heard the sound of keys jingling. Rome had found his means of escape. If Kate was still alive, Triton was about to lose her again.

As Triton struggled to shake the boxes off him, he heard Rome's footsteps heading away from him. The back door opened, then slammed shut as Rome made his escape. By the time Triton had weakly managed to get to his feet, Rome was gone.

Outside, Kate was being yanked back toward the lodge. Angela was unnecessarily rough with her, as if trying to convince Kate that she, Angela, would have won the fight even if she hadn't been armed. Like there was a chance in hell that would have happened. So far, Angela had only managed to hurt Kate when she was attacked unexpectedly, or when her hands were tied behind her back.

The gunfire had surprised Angela as well as Kate.

Triton's wife hoped that it had meant the cops had arrived, but feared it was just Rome finishing off the other members of his gang, as he did with Vescera earlier.

"Looks like it's just you and Rome now," Kate said, getting in another dig. "Wonder how long before it's just Rome."

As the shooting stopped, Kate saw Rome running out of the building toward them, pointing to the car that Kate had tried to get in earlier. The calm demeanor that Kate had witnessed in control all afternoon only faltered slightly as he ran.

"That's our ride!" Rome shouted as he pointed his gun at the car. "Time to go!"

Angela immediately pushed Kate in that direction. If the car was the goal, Kate was in no rush to get there. She went weak in the knees, nearly pulling Angela down with her, but the woman held firm. Angela yanked Kate back to her feet, but Kate refused to give in that easily. She was doing her best to slow them down, hoping that Rome's quick exit indicated that help was close behind him.

"Go where?" Angela asked as she struggled against Kate. "What happened?"

"Her Marine showed up. You believe that?" Rome said as he reached the car.

This new information stopped Kate in her tracks. "He's alive?"

She looked to the lodge, stunned. At first, she worried it was some cruel joke. But that made no sense whatsoever. It had to be the truth—if only to explain their need for a hasty exit. Kate's emotions were torn between joy, relief, shock, and a thousand other feelings that she couldn't begin to name. Her eyes swelled as she realized that she had always known deep inside that John would never let her down. Apparently not even death would stop the man she loved.

He was alive!

"Not for long," Rome said, spraying bullets into the propane tank and generator under the lodge.

Kate was horrified once again as she watched the wooden pylons being shot to bits. Sparks flew as the bullets tore into their targets. One of the hoses on the old gas tank was severed. It flapped wildly as gas spewed out into the air, catching on the sparks and igniting into flame.

Within moments, a fire raged under the lodge. Kate desperately hoped that John had had the opportunity to escape, but she couldn't see him inside. She was straining to look as the tank finally gave, exploding into a huge fireball that blew up into the building.

Through tears, Kate watched the building collapse in on itself. In the firelight she saw a shadow on the river. At first, she thought it might be John. As her eyes focused, she realized that it was a small boat. It looked like a police boat.

Kate wanted to scream, but words could not come out. She was paralyzed by what she was seeing. Part of her refused to believe that John was dead, but how many times could he cheat death in one day? She knew she had a shot at alerting the police officer, if only she could make herself heard over the small explosions that continued in the wreckage.

But she never had her chance.

Rome continued toward the car while Angela pulled Kate along, roughly. Before she knew what was happening, Rome had opened the trunk and was forcing her inside. Kate tried to fight back, but it was no use. Her legs slammed against the bumper as she toppled in. Luckily, she didn't hit her head on the frame and fall unconscious. She was bruised, but otherwise unharmed.

Rome slammed the trunk shut, leaving Kate in the darkened interior. Her mind was racing, but she was able to focus. Working in a hospital, she had heard many stories of tragic deaths. A few months earlier, a woman had died while locked inside a trunk. She had never realized that there was an emergency release right above her head. Kate did a visual search for a similar trunk release, knowing that most would glow in the dark. There was no sign of an escape mechanism.

Kate heard two car doors slam shut. Moments later, she could feel the tires peeling out on the gravel beneath her. Just because there wasn't a glow strip did not mean that there was no way out. But it wasn't going to be easy to find with her hands tied behind her back.

As the car bounced over the unpaved road, Kate did her best to feel along the trunk with her arms and legs. Any latch or lever would be located in an easily accessible spot, so it wasn't like she needed to dig into every tiny nook of the trunk. After a few minutes, it was clear that there was nothing obvious to grasp. It was also increasingly difficult to search as she was thrown about the small space.

Forgetting the potential latch, she took in the rest of the confined space. The trunk itself was empty, though she suspected there might be a compartment underneath the trunk floor with a spare tire and, possibly, a tire iron. However, repeated attempts to get under the flooring proved useless. As she felt the car pass from dirt to paved road, she finally gave up the search for an escape, deciding instead to conserve her energy.

Alone, in the darkened trunk of the car, Kate slumped onto her side as her emotions overwhelmed her. Once again, she felt the pain of having lost her husband. This time, she feared that it was for real. As she lay on the trunk floor, she finally gave herself permission to cry.

28

Triton heard the bullets slamming into the metal tank below him. He had already taken stock of the dangerous items beneath his feet. It wasn't difficult to imagine what Rome was trying to do. Triton looked down through the holes in the wood flooring to see sparks flashing underneath the boards. Rome was trying to take him out and get rid of any evidence in the process.

There was a bright flash as something ignited under the lodge. Flames snapped and grew, licking up through the slats under his feet. Triton ran for his life, trying to escape the billowing explosion.

He moved toward a window at the river-facing side of the lodge. When he was only steps away from the window, the flames burst into one huge explosion. Triton managed to jump just as the lodge was rocked by the enormous blast. A fireball chased after Triton as his body flew through the air. He could feel the heat wrapping around his body as the blast pushed him out the window.

The cool water was a shock to his senses, following the extreme heat that had been on his heels. Triton's body cut through the swamp as the massive fire lit the darkening sky. He swam away from the building underwater, hoping to avoid the debris as shards of glass and wood fell into the water around him.

When he could no longer hold his breath, Triton broke the surface of the water, taking in deep gasps of oxygen, his body racked with pain. Once he got his bearings, Triton saw that he was halfway between the lodge and land. He turned toward the parking lot and saw what he suspected was Van Buren's car spraying gravel as Rome raced away, taking Kate with him. Unable to hold in his pain any longer, Triton roared with fury and frustration.

"Out of the water!" a voice yelled behind him. It sounded as if someone was speaking over a loudspeaker. "Get out of the water! Now!"

Triton turned to find a lone police officer on a small riverboat. The loudspeaker was wholly unnecessary, as he had been pulling the boat up alongside Triton while he spoke. Exhausted, Triton simply nodded in compliance with the officer's request and swam toward the shore.

His muscles strained as he cut through the water to the riverbank. Even though he had continued his workout regimen while he was temporarily stationed in Germany, nothing could have prepared Triton for what his body had been through today. And it still wasn't over yet. He promised himself that much. He would take a moment to update the cop so he could call it in, but he was going to get Kate, with or without police assistance.

As Triton dragged himself out of the water, the riverboat cop beached his boat and jumped out with gun drawn. He looked to be several years younger than Triton and entirely inexperienced with the kind of day Triton was having. The cop kept his gun trained on Triton. It was possible that his hands were even shaking a bit. Triton didn't really blame him. It wasn't every day that someone witnessed an explosion like that. It was even more rare to find someone who had survived it.

But surviving explosions like that used to be an everyday activity for John Triton.

"Down on your knees!" the cop commanded. "Hands behind your head."

Triton complied with the officer's demands, dropping to his knees and remaining there as the cop crept toward him. It was taking longer than it should have because the young officer was being extra careful as he approached. Triton didn't blame the guy. He was just doing his job. Triton knew that he didn't have much time, but he would have less if he scared the cop into acting rashly.

"My name is John Triton," he said, hoping to move things along.

"Stay down. Don't move!" the cop said in return. He was obviously agitated. Triton understood. He'd felt the same way at the start of his training years back. The cop's adrenaline was pumping. He was trying to push away his fears. He took comfort in the routine, wanting to make this arrest by the books.

It was a rookie mistake—jumping to conclusions. Just because Triton was in the swamp and at the scene of the explosion, he became an immediate suspect. He knew he didn't resemble any of the crew that the police were searching for, but that didn't matter. The explosion trumped the diamond heist, and the cop had witnessed Triton smack dab in the middle of that. On top of everything else, now he had to convince the cop that he wasn't one of the bad guys.

The officer approached Triton with his gun in one hand and handcuffs in the other. Triton stayed on his knees, but tried to explain the situation. He was losing time.

"Please, they have my wife—"

"You have the right to remain silent," the cop said, ignoring Triton. "I suggest you use it."

At this point, Triton lost his patience. He'd never have the chance to explain what was happening if the officer wasn't even going to listen to him. The guy had obviously never learned that sometimes the rules can be set aside so you can get a handle on the situation. It was something Triton had figured out on his own years ago. But it was also something he didn't have the time to teach.

He didn't want to hurt the cop, but Triton knew this was his only chance to catch up with Kate. And he had to take it.

Triton found his opportunity when the cop went to cuff his wrist. In a lightning-fast series of nonlethal moves, Triton disarmed the cop, taking his gun and sliding one of the cuffs around the officer's wrist. He then dragged the man over to a partially sunken boat just offshore and attached the other cuff to the boat's ore ring. Triton knew he didn't have time to explain, so he kept it simple.

"They have my wife," he said to the cop and then left him there in the water, stuck to the boat.

Triton turned for a quick look at the road that Rome used to disappear. It probably took them to the highway, which ran along the river farther down toward the marina. Triton could follow them from the water. Without missing a beat, Triton ran the few steps down the shoreline and jumped into the patrol boat. He opened up on the throttle and the motor came to life. In a whirlwind of fury and desperation, Triton sped away from the burning lodge.

Angela had the pouch of diamonds open in her lap. She was sorting through them as if she was picking all the red M&M's out of a bag of the chocolate-covered candies. It wasn't exactly the smartest thing to do, considering they were in a cop's stolen car with a kidnapped woman in the trunk and half the state probably looking for them, but Rome didn't mind. He liked seeing Angela happy. When she was happy, she usually found a way to make him happy as well.

Angela raised a large diamond to her face. It sparkled as it caught the dimming light. "What do you think of this one?" she asked.

Before he could answer, she put it back in the pile

and picked up two others. She held them to her ears. "Or how about these? Can I have these, sweetheart?"

Rome looked at her with a sly smile. His mind was already thinking of a way to make them both happier. "I'm sure we can work something out," he said.

In the craziness of the day, Rome had almost forgotten what this whole thing was about. He was now a rich man. Far richer than the original plan had called for. Though the Marine had caused him no end of trouble over the past several hours, in a way, he had also managed to make Rome's life easier. With his entire crew—and the detective—gone, he could enjoy the money alone with Angela, minus a small split for the vehicle guy, Frank. Then again, if Rome could find a way to get Frank out of the picture as well, that would be all the more for him.

Angela leaned across the seat to kiss Rome as he drove. He kept one eye on the road as their lips met and tongues danced together. The kiss was more than just a thank-you for the diamonds. It was a promise of more to come.

Unfortunately, the kiss ended far too soon when the radio crackled to life.

"*Zebra Four, come in,*" a voice said. "*Van Buren, do you read?*"

Angela went back to her seat, slipping the last two diamonds back in the pouch. Rome was already checking the mirror for any approaching signs of trouble. As far as he could tell, they were practically alone on the road at the moment. A big rig was way down the highway behind them, but it wasn't much of a threat. They had passed a few cars earlier, but none of them had been the police. Rome pulled the car off the road, driving it behind a tall row of hedges that lined the highway, and cut the engine.

"*Zebra Four, come in,*" the voice insisted.

"What are you doing?" Angela asked, taking in their new surroundings.

"We gotta get rid of this car," Rome said.

"*Zebra Four, respond.*" The voice sounded concerned.

"Any suggestions?" Angela asked as she closed the pouch of diamonds and put it in her jacket pocket.

In the distance, they heard the loud blast from the horn of the tractor-trailer, as if in answer to Angela's question. It was approaching too quickly for them to catch it, but that didn't mean there wouldn't be other opportunities coming their way soon enough. He knew the highway was a major trade route for the area.

"We trade up," Rome answered as he popped his door open.

Kate felt the car pull off the smoothly paved road. Once again her body was jostled about as they rolled over uneven ground. At first she thought they were going back through the swamp, but the car stopped only moments after pulling off the highway.

Kate braced herself for an attack. She didn't have a weapon, but she knew this might be her last chance at escape. It was entirely possibly they had pulled over to dump her body.

The trunk opened, letting in the last light of the cloudy day. Though it wasn't bright, Kate still had to blink back the light as Rome pulled her roughly out of the trunk. He dragged her over to the road, where they remained concealed in the brush. Night was falling on the isolated highway. The occasional vehicles that passed were mostly mini-vans carrying soccer moms and their car pools.

Once again, Kate considered calling for help, but she was terrified of getting an innocent family with young children involved in her nightmare. As far as she could tell, it didn't look like Rome intended to kill her, for the moment.

Rome gave a nod toward Angela. Off in the distance, Kate saw the front cab of a truck coming down the road. It looked like they were planning to exchange their ride for some reason. Kate worried about what that meant, but she also saw it as an opportunity. She just hadn't figured out what to do with it yet.

Angela walked out of the brush, taking her black leather jacket off as she headed for the highway. She then adjusted her tight t-shirt to show off more of her waist, putting her body on display. Kate was disgusted to watch the woman, who seemed to be enjoying herself as she turned into a sexual predator.

Rome, however, was amused by the whole thing. "Watch this," he said, turning to his hostage. "You might learn something."

Kate wanted to spit in his face.

Angela took her position at the edge of the road,

with the truck cab barreling toward her. Kate could see her silhouette in the headlights. Her demeanor shifted as she became the quintessential damsel in distress, waving her arms to flag the semi down.

The truck driver must have seen her and liked what he saw, since Kate heard the unmistakable hiss of the air brakes as the cab came to a near-screeching stop. Kate thought about making a run for it, to warn the driver. She couldn't imagine that Angela was about to just leave the man stranded at the side of the road. Rome held tightly to Kate's arm, as if he knew what she was thinking.

Angela ran up to the passenger side of the cab. She jumped up on the running board and leaned into the open window.

"Thanks," she said, feigning helplessness. "I'm so glad you stopped."

Kate could hear everything from their position. She could also see that Angela was reaching for the gun stuck in her waistband behind her back. Once again, Kate considered a shout of warning, but that would probably just wind up getting both her and the driver killed. She knew that all she could do was watch and listen as the scene played out to its inevitable conclusion.

"No problem, little lady," the truck driver said with a lustful tone. "Happy to help."

"You are a lifesaver." Angela played it up. "I can use some help right about now."

"Why, sure," the man said as his tone changed from

friendly to what he probably thought passed for seductive. "I'll do somethin' for you . . . if you do somethin' for me."

"Right now?" Angela asked, teasingly. "Here?"

"Now's good for me," the truck driver said.

Kate couldn't see Angela's face, but she knew the woman was smiling when she pulled her gun and shot the truck driver dead.

Kate didn't even jump at the sound of the gunfire. It was as if she couldn't even be shocked any more with whatever new turn the day had taken. But just because the guy seemed a bit scummy didn't mean he deserved to die.

Rome pulled Kate out to the road and handed her off to Angela.

"Here, use these," he said, handing Angela a pair of handcuffs. Kate assumed that he had taken them off the cop whose car they had stolen. She wondered once again just how many people had died during their crime spree today.

Angela pushed Kate into the passenger's side of the cab, directing her to the small backseat. She slipped one of the cuffs onto Kate's wrists and started to untie her hands from behind her back.

"Don't even think about it," Angela warned as the bonds came loose.

At that same moment, Rome opened the driver's-side door and aimed his gun at Kate to underscore Angela's words. Kate went limp as Angela took her arm and handcuffed it to a metal rail in the backseat.

Once she was locked in, Rome holstered his gun. He checked to make sure no oncoming traffic was coming, then pulled the driver's dead body out of the cab. Kate watched as Rome slid the man out of the front seat and deposited him in the brush on the side of the road. In less than a minute, they were back on the highway with Rome at the wheel of the truck.

"So what's the deal?" Angela asked as they rode down the highway. "How far's the dropoff?"

"We'll hit it in no time," Rome replied. "And then we're home free."

Kate could only assume that what she'd just heard wasn't good news for her. If they were free, it meant there was no need for a hostage. Though it seemed that a lunatic like Rome was just as likely to let her go at the end of the day as kill her, she doubted that she'd be so lucky with Angela. That one would pull the trigger at the first opportunity. Kate turned away from them, looking vacantly out at the scenery as it passed by. She was running out of opportunities. She was running out of time.

29

Sheila Cohn had been regretting her decision to go camping for the past half hour. She should have known better when she agreed to take Dan. All of her friends had been telling her how different they were. Or, more specifically, what a loser he was. But she refused to listen. Considering all the hard-asses she had dated in the past, she was looking for a guy with a more sensitive side. As a result, she had found Dan.

Maybe now she needed to find someone in between.

Dan was walking beside her, continually slapping and scratching at real and imaginary insects.

"These bugs are eating me alive," he whined. "How much farther?"

"Not far," she replied.

"You said that like an hour ago," Dan insisted. "I'm sweaty. I'm itchy. I want to take a shower."

"You wanted to go camping," Sheila reminded him.

"I meant like a beach," he said. "Maybe throw a Frisbee. I forgot I was dating Lara Croft."

Sheila was getting tired of his crap.

Dan finally just stopped where he was. "I have to

take a leak. Can you check the map to make sure we're not lost?"

"We're not lost," she replied.

Dan didn't seem to care. He just handed her the map and went off into the trees to pee. Sheila looked at the map, but it only confirmed what she already knew. Sheila had been to this campsite several times before. She knew all the routes. She had even taken the path that ran along the highway, fearing that Dan would wimp out halfway through, and they'd have to hitch back to their car.

She called out to the trees, "It's just another mile or so to the campsite, okay?"

There was no answer.

When Sheila turned in the direction that Dan had gone, she saw him standing, frozen, at the edge of the weeds.

"Hey, what's wrong? You forget how to pee?" she asked as she walked over to him. As she approached, she saw his face had gone even whiter than usual.

"W-we need to call the police," Dan said. His voice was trembling.

"Why? What is it?" Sheila asked. She could tell something was seriously wrong. This wasn't his normal whininess. This was different.

Sheila followed his gaze into the weeds. There was blood all over the place. At first she thought they had stumbled across some dead animal. But as she followed the blood, she found that she was only partly right.

The CSI team arrived within minutes and had the

crime scene taped off. They had already been working their way south following the multiple crime scenes that afternoon. The trucker's body was neatly zipped up in the black body bag and being pulled out of the weeds on a gurney. State Trooper Mark Williams was overseeing this operation. Between State and the locals, they were already stretched thin. This was becoming one of the most vicious crime sprees in the history of the area.

Williams knew that the trucker's death had to be linked to the ongoing manhunt. Hopefully, they had their first real shot at finding the bad guys. The hikers' statements probably wouldn't help much, but simply finding the body had provided enough of a lead.

Williams clicked on his radio to send out an all-points. "Dispatch, we've got an ID on the dead trucker," he said. "Raymond Wayne Everett out of Houston, Texas. Commercial truck ID number is Niner-Whiskey-Four-Zero-Zero-Seven-Bravo-Two. Run a check on that A-sap. Over."

"*Roger that*," replied the voice from dispatch. "*Running it now. Over.*"

On the river, nearby, in the swamp, Triton listened in on the radio in the police boat he had acquired.

"*State patrol seven-one, this is dispatch. Over.*"

"*Go for seven-one. Over.*"

"*We have a positive ID on your vic, Raymond Wayne Everett. Last logged in driving a gray Peterbilt semi rig*" *with no trailer. A vehicle matching that description was last seen twelve miles southbound from your location."*

On that news, Triton throttled the police boat engine, sending it roaring down the river.

Triton raced down the river in the police boat. He knew it wouldn't be long before the entire force was after him for taking their property. The officer he had scuffled with surely would have reported the explosion before they had done their little dance. Other officers were probably already on their way to investigate and would find their buddy handcuffed to a boat in the water. After the initial ribbing, they would get down to business. If Triton thought it had been difficult enough to convince one cop that he wasn't the bad guy, he was going to be hard-pressed to explain things to an entire force after him for making one of their own look like a fool.

His need to get to Kate was even more intense than before, now that he knew that the police were probably after him as well. It would only get worse once they realized Van Buren had died in the explosion. No one would have known he was a dirty cop. They would have just thought he was a hero who died while trying to apprehend several fugitives. Somehow Triton had gotten himself in the middle of that mess too. Not that he had ever thought that getting Kate back was going to be easy, but now things had taken on a whole new—and considerably worse—turn.

The river was getting choppier as the winds were kicking up. The slow-moving storm grew closer as the sky darkened with night. Triton knew that the place that Rome had mentioned on his cell call earlier—Rita's—was on the water. The truck stop also had a pier with a gas station, where boats could dock. It was the kind of place where Rome could get in and out unnoticed, blending in with other travelers. It was especially easy for him to blend in now that he had a truck of his own.

The river ran closer to the highway as Triton neared Rita's. An occasional break in the trees allowed him a glance at the road. He kept an eye out for the truck cab he had heard described over the radio.

Triton eventually saw the sign for Rita's up ahead. It was right off the pier for the shoreline fuel depot that sat across from the restaurant. Triton knew it was faster to get to Rita's by the river than the road. Even though Rome had gotten a head start, he still had to work his way out of the swamp before he reached the highway. Triton suspected that they would be showing up any minute. He did his best to keep himself in control while allowing his rage to motivate him. It was likely that this was going to be the final showdown.

Rome pulled the semi into the parking lot of Rita's. Kate recognized the diner immediately. She and Triton had been to Rita's a couple times when they'd gone fishing with Joe and his assorted girlfriends. The diner looked like it was already getting busy. It was probably full of people who had decided to stop off to wait out the storm. If she could find some way to get inside, she knew that she'd be able to find help. But first she'd have to get the handcuffs off.

Kate examined the cuffs on her wrists. There was no way she was going to get out of them as easily as she had freed herself from the ropes earlier. She looked down the metal bar that she had been bound to. It seemed fairly secured to the cab interior. She gave a tug on the bar. It didn't budge. There had to be some way out of the truck cab—she just had to find it.

"It should be one of these," Rome said as he and Angela looked out over the cars in the parking lot.

"What's it look like?" Angela asked.

"Don't quite know, actually," Rome admitted. "I was just told we'd know it when we see it. Maybe it's on the other side of the diner. I think that's where the trucks and buses park anyway."

Kate assumed they were talking about another escape vehicle. At least this time they wouldn't need to kidnap or kill someone and take that person's car. Maybe they'd actually get out of this area without taking any more lives. Kate could only hope that hers was included in that scenario.

As they searched the parking lot, Kate looked out the window to see if she could find someone to help her. There had to be a police officer nearby. This was a fairly busy destination—someone would have to be covering it. Then again, she imagined the force was probably spread a little thin. Rome's crew had already left several crimes scenes in their wake.

Kate was beginning to lose hope as she realized

most of the people were already in the diner, since the dark clouds overhead looked like they were going to burst at any moment. It didn't look like there was anyone in the lot to come to her aid. But she was determined to stay optimistic.

Even while trying to remain positive, she still didn't expect to see what she saw in the trees along the edge of the river: a police boat.

Kate had thought the police were searching in the opposite direction. This was an unexpected turn of good fortune, the first one of the day. As her eyes focused on the boat, it just kept getting better.

John was standing behind the wheel. Alive. His face was set. His mind was on his task. It was clear that he was scanning the area, searching for her. Kate had never seen him on recon before, and she was impressed by the cold intensity of his face as he took in everything around him.

At this point, she was hardly surprised that he had survived the massive explosion back at the lodge. She was beginning to think she had married a cat with an inexhaustible number of lives at his disposal.

As if he could hear her mind calling out to him, John looked right into the cab of the truck. They locked eyes. She could feel his relief from across the distance as the truck continued slowly through the parking lot.

The silence in the truck cab pulled Kate's attention away from Triton. Rome and Angela were both focused on the parking lot. It was possible that either one of them could look beyond the cars to the river and see the police boat at any moment. They might not realize it was John, but they would know it was a problem.

Kate needed a distraction.

Her adrenaline was pumping. She had to act, and she had to act now. In one swift move, she lunged as far forward as she could. Leaning over Rome, she used her free hand to grab the steering wheel.

"Get this bitch off me!' Rome yelled to Angela.

Angela grabbed at Kate, who had locked her hand onto the wheel. As she was yanked away, Kate pulled at the wheel, sending the cab veering right and almost into a row of parked cars. Rome was forced to slam on the brakes as the tires screeched. Once the steering wheel was free, he righted the vehicle and continued through the lot.

Kate looked out the window to see that her plan had worked. John was already aiming the boat for the sandy riverbed and heading for her. It was only a matter of moments before she would be free.

She turned away so her kidnappers wouldn't know what she was looking at, and met Rome's fist in the process. The punch slammed her back into her seat. She was dazed, but it didn't matter. She knew that John would return the favor for her. Times ten.

30

Triton ran toward the semi as it continued past the parking lot. It was approaching a loading dock next to the garage, which provided Triton just the opportunity he was looking for. Seeing Kate again had given him the strength he needed. He was going to finish this once and for all. He would not let her down.

His plan was simple: Get Kate out of the truck. Kill whoever got in his way.

He heard Rome's voice carry out of the truck as he ran. "Waste this bitch, now!"

With redoubled energy, Triton charged toward the loading dock, breathing steadily as he ran. In three large steps he bounded up the dock and leaped into the air. Landing on the back of the cab with a thud, he could feel it swing to the right under the impact. Triton looked back as the vehicle continued forward. He may have been unarmed, but with the training he had, he wasn't exactly weaponless.

"What the hell was that?" the woman inside asked. Triton's approach hadn't been as stealthy as he had hoped, but he knew he didn't have that luxury with Kate's life in imminent danger.

He answered Angela's question immediately by dropping onto the running board and pulling the passenger door open. In one move he grabbed the woman and ripped her out of the truck. As they rode along the road adjacent to Rita's, he tossed her body aside as if it were a piece of garbage.

Before Angela could hit the ground, a bus heading in the opposite direction slammed into her. The bus driver reacted in horror as Angela's body crashed through the glass windshield and into the bus. The tempered safety glass imploded as it was designed to do, but it barely slowed the force of Angela's fall.

She might have survived, but for the fact that her spine snapped into the vertical safety bar with a deafening crack. Blood and diamonds spurted out of her clothing as it was torn into pieces, landing around the screaming passengers in the first few rows.

The bus swerved as the panicked driver brought it to a screeching halt, slamming into several cars in the process.

Rome let out a howl of rage that could have been for either Angela or the diamonds—or maybe both. He glared at Triton while doing his best to keep the truck cab on the road.

Triton ignored Rome for a moment, glancing back to his wife. She was sitting silently in the backseat, looking both horrified and relieved at the same time. He wanted to take her into his arms and tell her it was all over, but it wasn't quite yet. Triton still had to go through Rome before he knew she'd be safe.

Before Triton could reach across the seat, Rome made a defensive move, jerking the wheel hard and careening recklessly around the garage. Triton's body slammed into the side of the big rig, and the passenger door shut beside him, nearly taking his hand in the process. But he still managed to keep his grip.

The truck was now heading in the direction of the shoreline oil depot, a large warehouse that sat on the river. And it looked like it was getting bigger as the truck was picking up speed. Triton was having a hell of a time hanging on as the vehicle bounced offroad. He grabbed on to the wing mirror for support and used it to raise himself up to the passenger window. Not wanting to risk the swinging door again, he was going to take a more direct route and go through the only opening he could find.

Rome saw Triton's move. He countered by swinging the cab farther to the right in an attempt to slam Triton off the cab by crashing through a small wooden outbuilding. Triton held tightly to the cab frame as they burst through the wood structure.

Pain shot through Triton's side as he absorbed the impact, but he refused to let go. Wood splintered around him as the small building was virtually destroyed. He still kept his grip on the wing mirror, but nearly lost his footing.

Triton managed to regain his balance and started to make a second attempt on the window. But Rome saw the maneuver and swung the cab again.

The truck cab was approaching a second building.

This one was far more formidable than the last. Triton doubled his effort to pull himself into the window, but couldn't get enough traction on the side of the smooth metal door to propel himself inside. Giving up, he pressed himself against the side of the truck as it made impact with the building.

Sparks flew as the running board skidded against the outside of the concrete structure. Triton could feel the wall skimming against his back. If anything was sticking out of the wall—a windowsill or an awning—he would likely be cleaved in two. Luckily, the wall was smooth, and the cab took the brunt of the damage, keeping Triton relatively unscathed.

The truck quickly passed the building with little damage to Triton beyond some wear and tear on the back of his shirt. When Triton focused his attention back inside the truck cab, he didn't like what he saw; Rome was driving with a new determination, looking straight ahead.

Triton's eyes followed Rome's intense stare.

The crazy bastard was driving full out, heading directly for the wall of the depot.

Triton managed to lean halfway inside the cab. He tried to reach for Rome or the steering wheel, but they were both too far away for him to grab. In the back-seat, Kate was moving frantically, pulling at her arms. He saw that she was handcuffed to a metal bar. She was trapped. There was no way he could get her out of there before impact.

Kate froze as her eyes locked with Triton's. He tried

to silently give her the reassurance she needed as the truck slammed right through the wall of the building.

Triton was finally knocked off the side of the truck as the metal wall did what the earlier two walls could not. He landed on the hard concrete floor with the wind knocked out of him. All around him, the building cracked and debris flew as the semi plunged though a stash of oil drums that burst into flames.

"Gotta go!" Rome shouted to Kate in the now burning truck cab. In one insane instant he swung the driver's-side door open and leapt from the speeding cab. The truck continued to roll forward, plowing though the back wall undeterred.

The building exploded in front of Triton with a colossal blast that kept him pinned to the ground. He could only watch as flames and shrapnel engulfed the truck as it went airborne, crashing through the back wall of the depot, flying out of the building, and landing in the river.

Triton's eyes went wide with horror. As soon as the blast subsided, he was on his feet and running through the burning building, praying that Kate had survived the explosion. Machinery popped and crackled as a series of smaller explosions went off around him.

The truck cab was not totally submerged, but it was sinking quickly. Kate could still be alive, if only he made it in time.

He was nearly to the new exit when a wood two-by-four slammed into his ankles, sending Triton tumbling to the ground. As he registered what had happened,

Rome was quickly on him, continuing to pound Triton with the wood debris.

Triton took the first few blows before he reached up and pulled the wood out of Rome's hands, discarding it in the flames. He then popped up on his feet and traded punches with Rome, forcing the man into the heart of the building, keeping him away from Kate. Machinery and crates were now burning around them. It looked as if the raging fires of hell itself were raining down on them.

As the men fought, Rome grabbed a sledgehammer from a nearby crate and swung it at Triton's head. Triton was backed up against a metal standpipe. He managed to duck out of the way, but felt the wind as the weapon breezed over his closely cropped hair. The sledgehammer connected with the standpipe with a deafening clang.

Rome was slightly jarred by the impact, but it didn't slow him. Triton moved to get free of the pipe, but Rome kept coming. He swung the hammer again and again as Triton ducked and dodged out of the way. Triton could feel the heat behind him. He was moving toward a wall that was engulfed in flame.

Triton took smaller steps. He could feel the flames licking at his back. As Rome continued to swing his weapon, Triton dropped to the ground and kicked Rome in the knees. Rome screamed in agony, stumbling back.

Before Triton could renew his attack, Rome pulled another weapon from a nearby workstation. This time, it was a chainsaw. One flick of the switch set the deadly blade spinning.

Knowing there was no way to defend himself against the killer blade, all Triton could do was dodge the machine. It helped that Rome was having some difficulty maneuvering the heavy chainsaw.

Triton focused on Rome, forgetting the blade for a moment and watching the man's body indicate his intentions. With every twist of Rome's torso, Triton was able to counter-move and stay clear of the chainsaw. As Rome continued to come at Triton, the former Marine knew that he was running out of room.

Triton glanced back and saw that he was coming up on a counter that was built into the burning wall of the building. It was only another step until he could use the layout to his advantage.

Leaning back against the counter, Triton lifted his body and kicked the base of the chainsaw out of Rome's hand. It was a dangerous move, but luckily the weapon fell harmlessly out of the way, whirring to a stop several feet away from them.

The move also sent Rome back a few feet farther away from Triton.

With his enemy stumbling, Triton took a moment to look out the burning hole in the back wall. The truck cab was taking on water. If Kate wasn't already dead, she would be soon.

That thought was all Triton needed.

Triton launched himself off the counter and at Rome, knocking the man backward several more feet.

289

Triton landed punch after punch as he backed Rome into a small office built inside the depot.

The fifteen-by-fifteen room held little more than rusted filing cabinets and an old desk. The makeshift low ceiling was crackling with fire. Triton barely registered what was around him, all of his focus on finishing Rome.

His enemy tried to fight back, but Triton overwhelmed him, landing blow after blow. He finally ended it by smashing Rome through the wood support beam.

Triton pulled back as the fiery beams in the low ceiling came crashing down on Rome. In the brief moment of silence that followed, Triton could see that some of the flames were nearing another stock of oil cans.

Ignoring Rome, Triton ran for the new exit. He could feel the heat as the building exploded behind him.

Triton rode the explosion as he dove into the river, swimming with urgency in every stroke, as if his own life depended on it. Kate *was* his life, so in his reality, it was as if he were the one handcuffed to the sinking truck. When he reached the cab, he took a deep breath, filling his lungs with air, and went under.

It was dark under the water, but the light from the burning building was enough for him to see by. He moved along the side of the truck and looked inside the cabin. He could see Kate floating in the submerged cabin. Motionless.

Triton swam to the driver's-side door and slipped

inside through the open window. Seeing her wrist cuffed to the metal rail in the backseat, he reached for the bar. He tried again and again to rip the bar out of its bindings to set her free, not knowing if it was already too late.

It wouldn't move.

Making one last effort, he marshaled every ounce of his Herculean strength to wrench the bar out of the metal wall. He filled his mind with thoughts of the woman he loved to fuel his strength.

He saw her on their wedding day.

He saw her every time he had left her to ship out to some other far-off land.

But most importantly, he saw her jumping into his arms when he returned home for good.

That last image gave him the power he needed to break the rail free with a final tug. Triton slipped the handcuff off the rail and pulled Kate out of the truck with him. Together, they rose to the water's surface. Using his free arm, he pulled them both to the shore.

Triton rushed out of the water, carrying Kate in his arms. He quickly put her down on the riverbank, kneeling beside her to administer CPR, attempting to breathe life into her.

There was no response.

Rain fell softly as drops landed on Kate's lifeless face.

"C'mon, Kate," he pleaded with a strong whisper. "Breathe."

And still nothing.

"C'mon," he pleaded, almost in anger.

Kate moaned slightly. Her head shifted to the side, finally showing a sign of life. But nothing followed. Triton's lips lowered to hers once more with newfound hope.

Triton felt the harsh metal of a chain wrapped around his neck, yanking him roughly away from the love of his life. He knew that he should have confirmed that Rome was dead, but Kate simply hadn't had that luxury of time.

"Say hello to your wife for me," Rome said into Triton's ear.

Rome thought she was dead. And she may have been. Either way, Triton knew that if he let Rome win, Kate would surely die.

Once again, Triton found what must have been his absolute last reserve of strength. He raised himself upon his feet, pulling himself free of the chain and yanking it out of Rome's hands.

Triton spun on Rome and looped the chain around the man's neck. Without bothering to answer Rome, Triton lifted the man and flung him into the air. The chain went taunt as Triton snapped Rome's neck with a strong jerk.

Sirens sounded off in the distance, but Triton knew even if there was an ambulance coming, it would still be too late.

Triton returned to Kate's side, continuing with the CPR.

Nothing.

"C'mon, Kate," he pleaded with her again. "I love you."

He covered her mouth with his one last time, kissing her gently and holding her face in his hands.

He could feel Kate's chest rise as air flooded into her lungs. She broke their kiss, coughing with forced breath. Her eyes opened.

She was alive.

Triton's emotions ran the gamut of joy, relief, love, and a dozen other feelings. No rescue had ever been so satisfying. Nothing in his life had ever been more important. He held Kate tightly, silently promising that he'd never let her go again.

Police cars skidded to a stop all around them. The dome lights spun, casting an eerie light on them as doors swung open.

Triton leaned back, his eyes meeting Kate's. "Maybe we should have gone to the beach," he said.

Kate smiled as she pulled him toward her for one more kiss.

Not sure what to read next?

Visit Pocket Books online at
www.SimonSays.com

Reading suggestions for
you and your reading group
New release news
Author appearances
Online chats with your favorite writers
Special offers
And much, much more!